Force Field

Doug stepped closer and Page felt a force field, so strong that she knew that there was no breaking this electrical connection. He took one quick glance around, then gently put his hands on Page's shoulders. She felt herself melt into him again. This was no sneak attack. This was so right that Page wouldn't have cared if the entire class was standing around laughing at the strangeness of her pairing up with weird Doug.

When they both caught their breath again, Page saw that no one was standing around. Doug grabbed her hand as they hopped down the steps. "It's going to work," he said, almost to himself.

"Is it?" Page breathed hopefully.

Doug threw back his head and grinned up at the sky. "It has to work. It's that weird."

CLASS of '89

by Linda A. Cooney

Freshman

Sophomore

Junior

Senior

CLASS of '89

JUNIOR

Linda A. Cooney

SCHOLASTIC INC.
New York Toronto London Auckland Sydney

ISBN 0-590-41677-4

12 11 10 9 8 7 6 5 4 3 2 1   8 9/8 0 1 2 3/9

Printed in the U.S.A.   01

First Scholastic printing, October 1988

CHAPTER 1

"Bets, did you see this one?"

"What, Laurel?"

"This folder. I got it for you. It's about what you have to do to become a veterinarian."

"I already saw it. Um, thanks, though."

Betsy Frank hugged her knees to her chest. Somehow, as far as careers were concerned, she wasn't in the mood.

But she was supposed to be. She and Laurel Griffith were huddled on the library floor between two towering bookcases. It was like crouching in an alley. When Bets leaned over to peer around the corner, she saw scores of legs and feet crammed together in the center of the library floor. Day-Glo tennies mingled with high heels. Open-toed sandals bumped into polished wing tips. Feet tapped nervously, rocked, side-stepped, or lunged. They were all there for the Class of '89 Career Day, and everybody seemed really excited about it. Why wasn't she?

Laurel continued to browse eagerly through the stack of papers in her lap. "Look at this one, Bets."

"Which?"

"Look at all the things I can do if I study graphic arts. Advertising. Decorating. Even movie special effects." Laurel glanced up from her folder and gave Bets a gentle smile. Her wheat-colored, silky hair lay flat against the collar of her thrift-store dress, which was from the fifties, and printed with a gray and lavender geometric pattern. She had grass-green eyes that were a little shy behind wire-rimmed glasses. "You know, I didn't want to come to this," she confessed. "My dad made me. But now I'm kind of glad I came. It's interesting."

"I guess."

"You don't think so?"

"Oh, sure. It's interesting."

Unlike Laurel, Bets hadn't been forced to attend Career Day. She hadn't really thought about it at all. She'd just shown up. Maybe that was part of the problem. Career Day had turned out to be an after-school hoopla, where guests from different professions shared information about their jobs. Page Hain, junior class president, had set the whole thing up, and all those people attached to all those feet on the library floor seemed to be having a terrific time. Why aren't I? Bets wondered. Why am I so out of sync with everyone else?

"Illustrating posters, book and record covers," Laurel continued to read out loud. "Prod-

2

uct design. . . ." She pushed her glasses further up the bridge of her nose. The woven bracelet she'd worn every day for the last year inched its way down her wrist.

"What's that?"

"It means designing product packaging and labels." Laurel popped her head up and laughed. "Gee, maybe I could design the next Campbell's soup can."

"The what?"

"The soup can. You know, the red and white label on all those soup cans in the supermarket."

"You mean, um, that's a design? Like someone actually sat down and thought that up?"

"Sure, Bets. What did you think?"

"I just figured . . . I don't know . . . that's how soup cans always looked."

"Bets."

Bets rubbed her eyes. "I guess I never really thought about it."

Laurel went back to her papers.

Ugh, Bets thought. Score another one for dumbness. Along with a whole bunch of other things that were important, she just didn't think about stuff like who designed soup cans. Laurel seemed to think about everything artistic, and Bets's other closest friend, Micki Greene, thought about everything, period. As for boys, Bets's old buddy, Doug Markannan, would have probably thought about using the soup can as a percussion instrument or the lid as a part of a wind chime. Bets, on the other hand, just dumped her soup in a pot and ate it.

Laurel closed her folder and stuck it in her

book basket, which was already overflowing with sketch pads, calligraphy pens, a poetry book, some straw-textured blue wildflowers, and a pair of ballet tights. "Bets, I think I saw some other info about being a vet out there. Do you want me to help you find it?"

"I know where it is."

Laurel leaned over Bets to look. "Do you see Micki? Maybe she could get it for you."

Bets shook her head. "That's okay."

"Are you sure?"

"I'm sure." Bets felt a reflex go off inside. She didn't want to get Micki involved in this. Micki was too good at solving problems — especially for her best friend. Within minutes, Micki would be handing Bets more career information than she could absorb in a week. Besides, Bets already knew more than she wanted to know about careers in veterinary medicine. "It's too crowded anyway," she said as an afterthought.

"It is pretty crowded," Laurel agreed.

Bets sighed, but not loud enough for Laurel to hear it. This whole career thing had begun a month ago when, on a bleak March day, the counselor had assigned them all to pick a profession to investigate. Bets loved animals and had grown up on a ranch, so she decided on becoming a vet. She didn't give it another thought until she arrived at the library that afternoon and picked up the "Careers in Veterinary Science Fact Sheet." The first thing the sheet said was that she should be taking Advanced Algebra and Beginning Chemistry junior year. She should be getting mostly A's and B's. Bets was taking General Math 2 and no science at all. She was getting mostly C's. That made her perspective on careers a lot different than Laurel's. Laurel was truly talented. A great artist, she could draw a cartoon of your face in about two minutes with about three strokes and somehow it would always make you see yourself a little differently. Bets, unfortunately, felt she didn't have any talents. Not really. She was good with animals, but so what . . . that hardly qualified a person to be a vet. It took smarts to do that, and Bets wasn't feeling very smart today.

"I don't think I really want to be a vet, anyway," Bets said glumly, with a sound in her voice that said she had really made up her mind.

"I thought you did."

Bets wrinkled her nose. "No." She took her vet fact sheet and pretended to stick it in her notebook. When Laurel turned away, Bets slid the paper along the floor until the last white corner disappeared under the bookcase.

Bets brushed the dust from her freckled hands and laughed nervously, self-conscious that Laurel might have seen her. But Laurel was staring down the corridor now, away from the noisy crowd in the middle of the library. Her eyes had taken on a dreamy, fixed quality. Bets knew now that she could have screamed "fire" or waved a lighted stick of TNT. Laurel wouldn't have noticed. Jed Walker, Laurel's boyfriend, was making his way around the tiny cubicles along the back wall. A moment later he turned down their row and joined them.

"Hi," Jed said, crouching down next to Laurel and just barely smiling at Bets. He was a junior, too; handsome, with floppy dark hair, hidden eyes, and a moody way of shifting his shoulders. He wore a torn jean jacket that was smeared with paint and oil from the junk sculptures and motorcycles he worked on after school. Around his tanned wrist was a woven bracelet with a single knot. Exactly like Laurel's.

"Hi, Jed," said Bets.

Laurel kept staring, as if she were so happy to see Jed that it took her a moment before she was able to speak. He touched her knee and some wordless exchange passed between them. Bets clunked the heels of her cowboy boots together and hugged her own arms.

"What a scene," Jed commented, gesturing to the crowd.

Bets became aware of the noise again. It was that general-assembly hubbub, accented by president Page Hain making an announcement in her formal, icy voice. There was the far-off harmony of Doug goofing around singing back-up doo-wahs, probably with his new good friend Thompson Gaines, and the other guys. There was the occasional cough and the slap of books on tabletops, followed by Micki's familiar giggle. Still, it didn't sound as vibrant to Bets as it had before. Something about the intensity of Laurel and Jed's relationship always made the world around them a little dimmer.

"Was it as useless as you thought?" Jed asked Laurel.

Laurel's eyes stuck to his. She tugged on the hem of his jacket. "It was okay."

Jed stuffed his hands in his pockets. "Ready to go?"

They both stood and Bets peered up at them, disappointed that Laurel was leaving her. Of course Laurel had left her as soon as Jed had arrived.

"Laurel," Bets reminded her, "remember to ask your dad, you know, about spring break." Vacation was the following week, and Bets had invited Micki and Laurel to stay out at her family's funky old beach cabin.

"I will," Laurel smiled. Then she seemed to suck her words back in as Jed frowned and his blue eyes darkened.

"You can come, too, Jed," Bets assured him right away. "Lots of kids from the class are driving over." The beach was about forty miles from Redwood Hills. "At least, I hope they are. I think, um, Doug and some other guys are going to camp out — gee, I don't know . . . somewhere near the ocean, I guess."

Jed hiked his jacket collar up around his neck, and Bets felt embarrassed for even inviting him. Even though Laurel would sometimes join her and Micki for sleepovers or excursions to San Francisco, Jed was not the joining-in type. Finally he murmured something that was probably thanks. Then he and Laurel laced their arms around one another and, avoiding the crowd, took the long route to the library door.

" 'Bye," Bets whispered, mostly to herself. She stood up, stretched her long limbs, and watched them. Jed's arm rested on Laurel's delicate shoulder. Her arm was around his back, one finger hooked through his belt loop. They strode in step, their heads tipped toward one another, so that even their hair seemed to touch.

Bets sighed again, this time a really loud, forlorn sigh. Laurel and Jed always left Bets feeling heavy and left behind. She'd had a boyfriend for almost a year. L.P. Brubaker. She and L.P. hadn't been close the way Jed and Laurel were. Actually, by the end, Bets was only going out with L.P. because he was nice and he liked her. But there were moments with L.P., when they were kissing or dancing slow, when she felt something that must have been like Laurel and Jed. Bets felt important. She felt as if she and L.P. had something private and special that the rest of the world could have nothing to do with.

Still, it hadn't lasted. L.P. had started college last fall at San Francisco State, about a hundred miles south of the small town of Redwood Hills. Over Thanksgiving he'd come home and patiently explained to her that his life was changing. He was changing. He was two years older than she was to begin with, but college had really made the difference. He'd outgrown her.

Oh, well, Bets thought, things change. That's what her mother always said. You had to look forward to new things, which Bets knew she should try to do right now. Determined, Bets picked up her nearly empty notebook and made herself take a step toward the Career Day crowd. But her legs felt stiff, and besides, there was this awful, bricked-up feeling inside that stopped her. It was almost as if she were too heavy to move.

She shrank back against the bookcase. She could pick out Page Hain's efficient voice competing with Micki's relaxed, frothy giggle. More and more it seemed as if everyone in her class was changing as much as L.P. had. Page had started high school as a prima donna and a flirt, and now she was one of the most serious, respected juniors at Redwood. Micki no longer carried the weight of her class on her shoulders, but concentrated her sunny energy on a few good friends. Doug had changed from a geeky goofball to a very attractive, popular goofball. Even Laurel and Jed, the two loners, were no longer alone.

And yet Bets felt stuck. Stalled. In neutral, or maybe even in reverse. When she was an underclassman, she hadn't worried about being behind. It seemed that high school would go on forever, and there was unlimited time for catching up. But after this summer they would be seniors. Kids were already talking about majors and what they wanted to be. They were comparing PSAT scores and visiting university campuses, applying for special study programs and jobs that really paid. Meanwhile, Bets still brought her lunch in a brown bag. She read fairy tales. She baby-sat and didn't know that someone had designed the label on a can of soup.

"I want to go home," she mumbled to herself.

Head down, she almost squeezed her eyes shut when she entered the Career Day crowd. She let herself be jostled, even though she was strong enough to push in any direction. Micki was over at the "Careers in Teaching" table and jumped up to gesture that she was much too excited to leave and would call Bets when she got home. Bets continued to let the other students and teachers bump and chug her along. She passed the tables for careers in forestry, dentistry, engineering, computers, law, publishing, finance, social work, business, and the local army recruiter. She had that ton-of-bricks feeling again, and she was sinking.

When Bets finally got outside she was relieved that the sun was still high. There was a cool, ocean breeze and no more smell of ditto-master ink. The mountains stuck out clear as scalloped green felt, and she wandered aimlessly until she reached the main entrance to the school. She folded down onto the wooden bench, listened to the flag rustle over her head, and stared down at her strong, freckled hands.

She sat like that, motionless and heavy, until she heard a burst of sound that she hoped had something to do with Micki. But as the harmony came closer and she made out the bop-shoo-wops, she knew that it was Doug and his buddies again. There were four of them. Doug, his new friend Thompson Gaines (the third), and two boys from marching band, doing a sort of musical Marx Brothers out the double doors. Doug had a fat stack of Career Day papers tucked under one arm. He wore a baggy suit jacket over a tight T-shirt that said GODZILLA LIVES and, as usual, was lugging his saxophone case.

"Yo, Bets," he said between beats as they

strode by. He drummed the top of her head, then went right back to the oo-ahs, laughing and slapping palms with his buddies. The gang of them glanced at Bets, then kept on going.

Bets watched Doug's back for a few seconds. Wavy blond hair, rhythmic walk, long lanky legs. When they'd been underclassmen, all she'd had to do was smile at Doug and he'd have dropped anything, anyone to be with her. He'd have begged to walk her home, to carry her books. He'd have lingered on her driveway, teasing and tickling, trying to figure out how to kiss her again, like the way he'd kissed her freshman year. And all the time she'd have merely tolerated him or even rolled her eyes and pushed him away.

"Doug!" Bets cried, the life coming back to her tall, graceful body. She pulled herself up by the flagpole and raced across the front lawn, springing further and higher with each spongy step.

Doug turned back while Thompson and the other boys continued to snap their fingers and hum. When they were younger Doug had worn a scrawny ponytail that he called his rat-tail. Now the rat-tail was gone, and his hair was wavy blond all over. He slipped his sunglasses down to the tip of his nose and grinned at her. "What's the problem, Bets?"

The other boys stared, and Bets's brain jammed. "I, um, I guess . . . I wanted to know if you felt like, I don't know, maybe walking home with me."

He reacted with an are-you-serious? expression. "Bets, we live in opposite ends of town." He pushed the sunglasses back up on his nose and started jogging backward toward the parking lot. "Sorry," he called back, his buddies at his side, "we're heading downtown."

"That's okay." Bets hugged her arms again.

"See you tomorrow."

"Okay."

" 'Bye."

"Okay."

Bets knew they lived on opposite ends of town. She'd figured the guys were heading downtown. It was just that last year, that wouldn't have made any difference.

CHAPTER 2

"YAAAHOOOOOOO!"

Micki Greene could almost taste spring break. Sure, there was still another week of school. But over the weekend it had rained, followed by blinding white sunshine and a rainbow that stretched from Capitola Mountain to somewhere way over in Cotter Valley. On Monday, when Micki trotted down her hill toward school, she could smell the first flowers, fresh-turned garden soil, and spicy eucalyptus. The sun made her eyes water and her cheeks hot. She bolted into a run and let out a big, happy yell.

"WHEEEEEE!"

She plopped onto the bus-stop bench and watched the traffic zoom by, letting her imagination leapfrog from last week's Career Day to Bets's cabin at the beach, to what they would cover in her next five days of Algebra 3, Botany, Spanish 4, English Lit., and Debate. Her busy head hopped with debate strategies, algebra problems, and conjugated verbs *en Español*. By the time she saw Bets swerve around the corner, it took her a moment to recognize her longtime best friend.

"BETS!" Micki called, shooting up from the bench and waving.

Bets tipped up her chin in response, then checked behind her as she crossed the traffic on her rusty blue Schwinn. Bets's freckled face had a new way of frowning, Micki realized, and she was starting to bite her lip a lot. She used to look as fresh and unmarked as a baby, but lately her doe eyes were wary, and there was tension under her healthy pink skin.

"Have you been here long?" Bets asked, scraping her foot along the curb until she stopped and got off the bike.

"Nope," Micki smiled. "Just got here."

"I didn't mean to be so late. I, um, forgot my dumb history book. I had to go all the way back and get it."

"Bets, it doesn't matter. We have plenty of time."

"Really?"

"Really. No problem."

"Okay."

They walked to the corner, Bets dragging her bike and Micki leading the way with her books and manuals and dictionaries purposefully stowed under one arm. The older Micki and Bets got, the more different they became in style and appearance. Even though Micki didn't have to be the center of attention every second anymore, she had an ever-increasing taste for eye-popping colors and flash. Today she wore a short pink skirt, hightops, a turquoise turtleneck, and print suspenders. Her pecan-colored hair was knotted on top with wisps streaming down her neck and face. As Micki's taste became bolder, it seemed that Bets was more and more content to fade into the scenery. Bets's beige cords were a little sloppy. Her cowboy boots were scuffed and her untucked shirt was the same color as the frame of her bike.

Micki waved to other juniors cruising by in a car pool as they crossed Redwood Boulevard and headed down the straight stretch toward school. "Isn't it a great day?" She swung her books and squinted up at the sun.

Bets, who was usually the first one to babble on about flowers blooming, trees budding, or calves being born, merely shrugged.

"I just hope we have good weather at the beach. I can't wait."

Finally, Bets smiled. It was as if the thought of somewhere away from Redwood High restored some of her old even-tempered ease. "Do you think lots of kids will come?"

"Why not? Look how many showed up last year. Doug said a bunch of guys are camping with him again. I guess even Thompson is going to rough it — if you can believe that." Micki rolled her eyes and nudged Bets with her shoulder. Neat, preppy Thompson Gaines III was often the object of jokes between Micki and Bets.

"Are you really sure Doug is still going to

come?" Bets asked again after they'd walked another block. The campus was in view now. Tall redwood trees. Boxy classrooms. The rows of outdoor lockers, connected only by a roof awning. The red and blue Grizzly mascot on the side of the gym and the line of buses and cars squeezing into the parking lot.

"Of course Doug will be there." Micki laughed. "Whether we like it or not."

Bets ruffled her hair, which was cut short this year; short and very straight. "I just thought maybe . . . I don't know . . . everybody would stay here. Except me and you, and maybe Laurel. You know, I heard about Page Hain's spring break ideas, all that stuff she planned. I thought lots of people might stay here in town to do that instead of going away to the beach."

Micki felt her jaw clench. "I heard about that, too."

Page had organized an impressive list of spring break activities in Redwood Hills, probably inspired by the leadership conference she'd attended the previous summer.

"I kind of couldn't believe it," Bets mumbled.

"Me, either. She announced it right in the middle of Career Day."

"I guess, um, I'm glad I left kind of early."

They walked more slowly alongside the chain-link fence that separated the sidewalk from the school's backfield. Micki had been very aware of Page at Career Day. She'd waited to get information from the "Careers in Law" table, then had backed off when she saw Page there

16

first. The same had happened at "Careers in Government," until Micki ended up at the teaching display, which actually turned out to be interesting, too.

For two years, Micki and Page had been pitted against one another. Page had taken Micki's place as class leader and it sometimes seemed that the Class of '89 crowd had been split down the middle: Michelle Greene supporters on the one hand; Page Hain followers on the other. Last summer Micki had caught herself making a list of exactly who had joined each side. But she'd shredded the paper before she ever compared totals. It was a dumb thing to even think about, she knew now. Unproductive and dumb. She wasn't getting caught up in a rivalry with beautiful Page Hain ever again.

Micki and Bets stepped onto the high school's backfield. The ground was still gooey from the weekend rain, and it smelled of fertilizer.

"I–I just thought," Bets stammered, "I could do another big spaghetti dinner, you know, like I did at the beach last year, on the weekend before we go back to school. But if there aren't very many people, if everybody stays here. . . ."

"They won't," Micki insisted. "Everybody'll still come."

Bets didn't look convinced.

Now Micki felt a pop of real anger. It was okay for Page to steal some of her thunder — Micki was just as happy to be out of the storm for a while. But with Bets it was different. Bets seemed insecure lately. Down on herself. Especially since things had ended with L.P. It seemed as if Bets was afraid that everyone was about to go off and leave her.

"Everybody remembers that great spaghetti dinner," Micki reassured Bets. "Nobody will want to miss it if you do it again."

Last year, spring break had been a triumph for both of them. It had followed a rough winter for Micki, but vacation had turned things around. Kids had camped out, slept on Bets's porch or stayed with Kevin Michaelson, another classmate whose parents had a fancy new beach house in Arch Cove. Others drove over from Redwood Hills and back each day. They played volleyball, swam even when it was freezing, made bonfires, and ended the week with Bets's Spaghetti Dinner for Thirty. It was exactly what spring break was meant to be.

"I bet everybody stays in town this year," Bets moped, leaning on her bike and kicking the grass with her heel. "Even Doug."

Micki couldn't stand this much longer. She circled around in front of Bets, dumped her load of books in the bike basket, and rested her hands on the handlebars. Bets peered at her from under her bangs, her brown eyes sad and a little startled.

"Bets, have you read those notices Page put up? Did you hear the announcements?"

Bets shrugged.

"Do you know what Page has planned for spring break?"

Bets shook her head hard, like a little kid.

"I'll tell you." Micki counted Page's events

on her fingers. "A lecture about prepping for the SAT's. A seminar in how to decide on a college. That trip to visit U.C. Berkeley. First-aid and CPR class, and something about how to find a summer job. Doesn't all that seem a little weird to you, Bets?"

"I don't know."

"Well, I do." Micki was picking up steam. "I think that Page is trying so hard to be Miss Serious Leader, that she forgot one important thing."

"What?"

"That the whole point of vacation is to take a break from school and have a good time!"

Slowly the corners of Bets's mouth lifted. Then her shoulders started to jiggle. When Micki poked her, she broke into a full-fledged laugh.

"Gee, maybe, um, we should stay right here, at school all week," Bets chuckled. "Not even go home to sleep."

"Live in the library."

"The science lab."

"In Crabner's English class."

The mention of Mrs. Rabner — a teacher nicknamed Crabner because she was so humorless and nasty — sent them both into hopeless giggle territory. "We could just stare at our report cards," said Micki.

"We could be just like Page and never have a good time!"

They were flying now. Bets gliding on her bike, over the rocks and the bumps and the squishy mud. Micki raced beside her and they grinned at each other. This was like the skate-board races they used to have, or the times when fearless Bets had taken a terrified Micki horse-back riding. Both of them were giddy and goofy, being noisy and making people stop and stare.

Finally they reached the hallway outside the drama studio. Micki took back her books and they parted. Panting and smiling, Bets headed for the bike rack, while Micki hung back near the door of her first-period debate class.

"Meet me at lunch," Micki called.

"I will!"

"Whoever gets there first grabs a table."

"Okay."

"Maybe after school we'll go shop for new bathing suits!"

Bets waved and rode away.

Her spring cheer bubbling up again, Micki marched into Mr. Steinberg's class, a messy room with big windows, and walls covered with debate schedules and articles clipped from *The Wall Street Journal*. There was still time before the bell, and Steinberg was busy copying some-thing in two long columns on the blackboard.

Micki sat down behind Doug. She still couldn't figure out why Doug had enrolled in this class. Steinberg's first period was beginning debate, for kids who might eventually want to join the competitive squads, or just have prac-tice in framing arguments and expressing them-selves. Debate was an obvious choice for ambitious types like herself, Page Hain, and

Doug's pal Thompson. But Doug was usually more interested in the latest jazz release than in arguing the English parliamentary system versus the checks and balances of American government.

Micki ripped a piece of paper out of her notebook, wrote "beach blanket bozo, be there," folded it into an airplane and pitched it at the back of Doug's blond head.

"Ow!" Doug complained, clapping his neck as if he'd been bitten by a bug. He put down the war novel he'd been reading and turned around. When he saw Micki, he took a wad of pink gum out of his mouth and smooshed it on top of her notebook. "For you."

"You're so kind."

"That's me." Doug flipped all the way around in his chair until he sat facing her, with his arms crossed over the backrest. "This book is great." He tapped his paperback on her desk.

Micki leaned down to look at the title and he lightly whapped her on the top of her head. "Ow."

"One good turn deserves another."

"Doug, listen. I have to ask you something." Micki glanced around the room. Mr. Steinberg was chalking out something about team debate strategy and a new topic for after midterms. Thompson Gaines was striding in, looking predictably un-California in his button-down shirt, madras pants, and deck shoes. Perfect Page hadn't arrived yet.

"Mick, I'm listening," Doug reminded her.

He'd opened her notebook and was unzipping the sack that held her calculator, pencil sharpener, and flash cards.

She zipped it back up on his finger. "Are you going to the beach or not?"

"I told you I was going. I think you're getting senile. Stay away from that cafeteria chili."

"Doug, I just asked because Bets is worried that nobody'll come."

Doug frowned, pulled out his finger, and examined it for damage. His silence told Micki that Bets might be right. A lot fewer people probably would show up at the beach this year. Doug also got that funny, nostalgic look he got these days when someone mentioned Bets. "People *are* talking about all those events Page has planned in town."

"Great." Micki thought of asking Doug what she should do to cheer Bets up. She knew how Doug used to adore Bets. And that somewhere around the end of sophomore year his adoration had faded away. But before she could bring it up, Thompson dropped his bony frame onto Doug's desk. Thompson always managed to intrude when Micki and Doug had something important to discuss.

"You're so predictable, Thompson," Micki taunted.

He grinned. He had short curly hair and a smug smile that reminded Micki of David Letterman. "Why, thank you."

She quickly scrunched up a piece of notebook paper and threw it at him.

Thompson caught it in midair. "We're in a

rambunctious mood this morning."

Micki scrambled through her stack of books until she found her English dictionary. "Rambunctious," she teased, thumbing the pages. "That's another big word, Thompson. You just keep coming up with them. I'd better look it up."

"Hey, Thompson," Doug interrupted, "we're still camping at the beach aren't we?"

Thompson opened the paper Micki'd pitched at him and examined it. He seemed a little disappointed to find that it was blank. "Yeah. You have to teach me survival techniques."

"That's assuming you survive until then," bantered Micki.

The bell rang and Thompson stood up. "We should probably come back by the final weekend, though. I just heard that Page Hain is having a party."

"*What?*" Micki demanded, pounding a fist on her desktop. Steinberg was holding up his hands now, telling them to settle down. He was giving Micki a particularly annoyed look, but she felt like jumping up and screaming. A party! How dare Page throw a party! This wouldn't be just any party, either. Page's family owned the biggest, showiest winery in the whole area. Bets's spaghetti dinner was sunk. It wouldn't matter that Page was about as much fun as a barrel of ice chips; no one would miss a fancy Hain party.

"Page said to tell the whole class that they're invited." Thompson grinned again, sidling over to his desk. "So I suppose that even includes you, Micki Greene." Thompson gave her his toothy Letterman smile again, tossed back the crumpled paper, and dropped into his seat.

"Oh, boy," Micki grumbled. That was another thing about Page this year. She was so sensitive about being taken for a snob that she practically invited the entire class when she went to the shopping mall.

"What, Mick?" whispered Doug. He was facing front again, but talked to her out of the side of his mouth.

"Page."

"What about Page?"

"She's such a . . . a. . . ."

Just at that moment, Page made her entrance. She wore an off-white skirt and blazer and carried a little briefcase, stopping in the doorway just long enough for the entire class to admire her ice-crystal beauty. Her long dark hair was tied back with a pale, thin ribbon and her gray eyes glanced briefly at Micki. Micki waved — a clawlike, mocking wave, one she'd give to a spoiled two-year-old. Not sure how to react, Page tried to smile. But her picture-perfect face wouldn't quite obey her. Then Doug squinched up his face in a demonic, exaggerated wink which made Page go even paler and rush to her front-row seat.

"I know it's Monday, but do you think you can all get settled?" Mr. Steinberg asked sarcastically. He pointed to the board. "Everybody copy this down while I take roll."

Instead of writing, Micki watched Page for a moment. Page quickly took out her leather-covered binder and started copying as if her life depended on it. Doug was still making faces, and Thompson was smirking, but Page was much too diligent to notice any longer. Finally Micki kicked Doug under his chair and went to work herself.

Micki took out her ruler and made two even columns. She stared and copied, but a moment later she looked down at her paper and a surge of alarm jolted her. She wasn't copying Mr. Steinberg's team debate format. She was making another kind of comparison. Bets's spaghetti dinner versus Page Hain's party.

"Cool it, Micki," she mumbled to herself, as she drew a huge "X" across her paper. She couldn't afford to get into this again. She wasn't getting strung out over Page's party or vacation or anything else, short of nuclear war. She was going to be mellow, easygoing, take-things-as-they-come Micki. It was simple. She wasn't going to let Page Hain, or anyone else, drive her crazy.

CHAPTER 3

"Laurel, what are you reading?"

"A catalogue."

"For what?"

"College. The University of California. Berkeley."

"What does it say?"

"Do you want to see it, Jed?"

"Nah. Boring. No way."

Laurel slowly closed the catalogue and buried it among the sketch pads, pens, and comic books in her basket. Visions of art museums and tall buildings, dormitories and wide lawns went away. Instead she saw Jed. Beautiful Jed, lying on his stomach. Close. His chin was perched on his fist. A twig was suspended from his dark hair. His deep blue eyes watched her, filling her with that hazy, floating feeling she got just from looking at his face, his shoulder . . . his graceful, paint-stained hands. She reached until his fingertips met hers and they intertwined fingers and palms. They held on hard.

"I love you," Laurel whispered.

Jed's eyes closed. He let her words run down his face like warm rain. "I love you, too."

They were on the bank of a small creek that trickled along the back of the Hain family vineyard. Up one hill were rows and rows of skinny grapevines evenly spaced and tied to wooden stakes. Beyond was the dirt road that led from the highway to the three-story Hain house — Page's house. Much closer was the squat trailer home with the metal awning where Jed lived with his uncle, who worked on the vineyard for Mr. Hain.

Jed let go of her hand to crouch over the edge of the water. Last winter's melted snow ran fast over the stones. When he picked up a rock and pitched it to the bank on the other side, Laurel scooted up next to him, smoothing her face against his soft flannel shirt and feeling the hardness of his back underneath. It was Friday, just after school, and the sun was shining as if it were midsummer. It was going to be gloriously warm for spring vacation.

"I finally got graded on my sculpture today," Jed told her, leaning his head back.

"From Foley?"

Jed nodded. Turning back to the creek, he picked up another stone, examined it, and sent it skipping.

"What did she give you?"

"B."

"That's good."

"It's not great."

"Foley never gives A's," Laurel said, even though she knew that wasn't quite true. Mrs. Foley was the advanced art teacher at Redwood, and Laurel had talked Jed into taking her class. They were in different periods since Jed took Sculpture and Mixed Media, while she took Painting and Drawing. One of the few things they didn't do together.

"She's given you an A," Jed said.

"Once. Maybe twice."

"She gave Paul O'Conner an A for that lame computer media thing."

Laurel wrapped her arms around Jed's neck and dug her chin into his shoulder. She plucked the rock out of his hand, tossed it. It thunked into the water and left a ring. "So?"

"So, with something like art, teachers don't know anything. It's something that can't be taught."

"That isn't what my dad says."

"Yeah, well . . . your dad."

Laurel's father, who was divorced from her mom before Laurel started Redwood, had just finished going back to grad school and had a new job with a software company. He used to be a teacher and was very big on higher education.

"What famous artist went to art school?"

"I don't know."

"Picasso?"

"Did he?"

"Van Gogh?"

"No way."

"Edward Hopper?"

"I don't know."

"I don't know, either." Jed smiled, one of his rare magical smiles. "I think people who fill out applications on the inside of match books are the only ones who go to art school."

Laurel jumped up behind him, threatening to push him in the water. But Jed pulled her back down until she was lying across his lap, the bright sun in her eyes. He pulled her in, kissing her. The sun and the gritty dirt softened, blending into the feel of Jed's hair, his mouth, and warm skin. Soon everything outside Laurel shut down, and everything inside was tuned to Jed.

This was the place they'd discovered last summer. Their place. It was far enough from the grapes and the Hain house that no one from the vineyard bothered them, and separate enough from the trailer that Jed's uncle hardly knew they were there. It was also the place where they could avoid Laurel's father, who'd been harping lately about how she and Jed spent too much time together.

They kissed until they were both foggy and lost. Laurel thought it was almost like twirling too many times when she was a kid. Only a noise from the upper road drew them apart and, for a second, Laurel felt so loose and drifty that she didn't quite remember what planet she was on, let alone what piece of property. Then she saw a couple of cars chugging up the dirt road toward Page's house and realized that the sound that had pried her and Jed apart had been a car horn.

Jed squinted at the road and scrambled up.

The magic privacy of "their place" had been invaded, even though the cars were at least a half acre away. "What's going on?"

"Something to do with Page, I bet." Laurel stood, too, her arm twisting around Jed's. Two more cars turned off the highway, including a white convertible that belonged to Cindy White, a girl in their class who was a devoted Page Hain follower. That's when Laurel remembered seeing a sign at school about a meeting to discuss Page's spring break activities. Page had lots of meetings this year. Even when Page walked down the hall at school she usually looked like she was in a meeting, swinging her briefcase, surrounded by six or seven other juniors. Page seemed to be a totally different person from the loyal, angry, funny girl Laurel had been friends with freshman year.

"Yeah. It's kids going over to Page's for some meeting about vacation," Laurel told Jed. She didn't ask if he would be joining any of Page's activities. Jed prided himself on not being a joiner. And besides, it would have been weird for him to walk across the vineyard from his run-down trailer to her fancy house. Even though Jed and Page lived on the same spread of land, they pretended as if they'd never met one another. Actually, when Laurel ran into Page at school now, they acted much the same way.

"Your dad's cool about vacation, though," Jed made sure, turning away from the cars to look into her face again. "He hasn't mentioned having to go see your mom again?"

"He dropped it." Laurel shrugged. "I think

my mom doesn't care if I come see her anymore."

"Sounds familiar."

"So we're safe."

"Good."

She slid her arms around his waist and moved closer, pressing away the skittishness she felt every time vacation rolled around. In the year that she and Jed had been together, they hadn't been parted longer than the weekend trips Laurel took to visit her mom. For her first two years of high school Laurel had been shuttled back and forth for the full length of every vacation. But since her mom had had a baby that fall, it was almost as if Laurel had been replaced and forgotten. Unlike Jed, who brooded sometimes about how his mom didn't care about him, Laurel was relieved not to spend a third of the year with her mother and stepfather anymore. It was much too confusing.

And besides, she hated being away from Jed. Even the weekends away last summer had been physically painful, as if her body had been emptied of some vital ingredient. When she wasn't with Jed it seemed as if every second ticked at her. Time moved more slowly than during the most deadly lecture or the longest car ride.

"So I'll go to the beach with Micki and Bets. Like I did last year." Laurel tugged on his jacket. "And you can sneak over and see me."

"Like I did last year."

Laurel laughed. "My dad thinks it's great that I'll be having a week away from you. He made a big deal out of it."

Jed flinched. "I can imagine."

"Jed," Laurel prodded. His shoulder had tensed in that moody way of his and he'd turned away from her.

"Yeah."

"What's the matter?"

"Nothing."

"Jed."

"Your dad."

"What about him?"

"He still thinks I'm a lowlife, or something."

"He does not."

"Oh, yeah?" Jed went back to the creek, angrily whipping open the laces on his tennis shoes, which were so coated with paint and glue that no one could tell their original color. He tossed the shoes onto the rocks and waded, not bothering to roll up his jeans. Then he kicked the water and sent out a long, sudden splash. "I'll show him, though. I will."

Laurel scrambled to kick off her lace-up boots and ran into the water with him. She held up her antique skirt, and the cold made her whole body go stiff. She balanced over the rocks, ignored the sharp stings on the bottom of her feet, until she was standing next to him. Shoulder, elbow, hip, thigh lined up. "I wish we could go away. We will one day," she said, hoping to distract him with one of their favorite pastimes — making up the perfect place where they would go when they were on their own.

"Just you and me," Jed mumbled.

"Where?"

He shrugged.

"We're in Vienna," Laurel improvised. Neither of them knew anything about Vienna, but she liked the sound of the name.

"Vienna. What does it look like?"

"You tell me, Jed."

He began to relax. "It has alleys with junk."

"Yes."

"Perfect junk for sculptures and perfect alleys for motorcycles. And no one speaks English."

"Our studio is on the top floor and it has huge windows that you can open and then walk right out onto the roof and watch all the people walking down below. And I grow flowers up there, and paint out there most of the time."

Jed's face took on the hopeful quality it always did when they played this game. "Except when it snows. But it hardly ever snows. Just on Christmas. And when people come to buy my junk sculptures we have a big chalkboard for them to write down how much they want to pay. Because we never talk to them."

"But they don't care that we won't talk to them. Because they pay us so much money, because we're famous."

"So famous that people wait in the snow just to come in and meet us."

Laurel laughed. "And they don't care that we still won't talk to them."

"We're even famous for that, for being the artists who only talk to each other."

"And people line up all around the block to see the stuff we make . . ."

"And when we don't feel like letting any more people in, we just shut the door!"

Jed suddenly swept his arm around her and pulled her down. Then they were both laughing, not feeling the cold water, or the stones or pointy twigs. And soon they were kissing again and there was no more father or house or sky or anything.

The cars continued to chug up to the road, but out behind the elegant Hain house, Page was avoiding her meeting. Avoiding her responsibilities, her faithful followers, her serious agenda and studious plans.

Instead, she stood out on the back deck, a big sun hat protecting her fine pale skin. She saw those two patches of color out there beyond the trailer and knew that they were Jed and Laurel. Whenever the weather was good, she saw them. The foreman grumbled that they hiked, lounged, kissed, out there on *Hain* property. He'd even complained to her father about it. But Page had urged her father to let it pass. She didn't care about trespassing. She thought that Jed and Laurel were guilty of another crime. Well, not really Jed. Just Laurel. In the year that Laurel had been in love with Jed, Laurel hadn't once come up to the house to say hello to Page.

"Page, will you get in there," demanded a taut, smoky voice.

Page turned around, startled. It was Whitney, her older sister, who was a senior and sick of anything having to do with high school.

"I'm coming."

"I can't believe it," Whitney complained, tossing back her dark hair. It frightened Page how much they looked alike. "You invite all those drippy high school kids and then leave me to entertain them."

"Whitney, I'm not leaving you with anything."

"Well, I'm not taking care of them."

Page tried to keep her temper under control — that terrible temper that was like a boiler running too hot. The last thing she needed was for her classmates to find her in a hair-tearing fight with her older sister. She willed herself to stay calm. "I don't expect you to, Whitney. Don't worry. I'll be in in a minute."

Whitney pouted and huffed. She whined. She rolled her eyes. Finally she backed off and left Page alone.

Page leaned onto the porch railing, breathed in the smell of grapes and dust, and let herself relax, as much as she ever relaxed these days. When they had been younger, Whitney never would have been the one to back down first. She'd have intimidated Page, embarrassed, and bossed her. Page had finally gained the confidence, the will, to stand up to her snobby sister.

Page had found out that when she put the force of her will behind things, she could achieve amazing results. She'd willed herself to be taken seriously at school. She'd avoided social games and romances, silliness and jokes. Instead she'd worked and thought and struggled and strained. And she'd done it. She'd proved that there was more to Page Hain than a rich family and a pretty face.

There was only one problem. Page had

worked so hard to create this persona for herself that she couldn't remember who the real Page was anymore. If there ever had been a real Page. All she knew was that there was something like another person inside her, threatening to burst out. And the more fiercely Page worked, the more serious she became, the harder that other person challenged her by putting the nuttiest thoughts in her head.

That was why Page was out here on the porch, rather than in with her classmates. She knew they all were waiting for her, but she had those crazy thoughts again. Lately she got these insane ideas right before she would get up to do something important. For an awful, unsettling moment she would be sure that, just at the worst possible moment, when all the eyes were on her, she was going to stick out her tongue, make pig noises, babble nonsense, giggle like a fool.

Of course, none of those things had ever happened. When the moment came for Page to walk in front of her classmates, she always did what she was supposed to do with dignity and control. But still, the images lingered. They made her heart thump and brought the blood to her face.

The answer, Page told herself, was to will them away. Just like she willed away her hurt about Laurel, her anger at her sister, her loneliness, and her doubt. Page clenched her fists. She pasted on a smile, told herself that everything was going to be just fine, and willed herself to go inside.

CHAPTER
4

Spring break.

Sandy towels. Gulls squawking. Sea-salt smell, and hot, stingy places on your skin where the sun had been for the first time that year. The even rumble of the waves and the competitive cries from the Redwood High volleyball game going on in the middle of the beach.

"Spike it, Bets! Spike it!" Micki yelled across the sand to the makeshift volleyball court. Bets, the only girl in the game, had leapt into the air with her fist poised over the net.

PUFFFTTTTT!

Instead of slamming the ball with her considerable strength, Bets pulled up at the last minute, waited, and politely returned the volley with a lilting, upward motion. Her freckled face had that tense look again under the thin layer of sunburn.

Thompson Gaines III was right there. Waiting

on the other side of the net in his plaid shorts, polo shirt, and sunglasses hanging from a thick red cord. His nose was coated with a neat triangle of zinc oxide.

THWACCKKKKK!

He jumped and slammed the ball back so fast that Bets didn't have time to cower. Her whole team — which included Doug, swimmer Kevin Michaelson, senior Greg Kendall, and two other boys, watched the volleyball dive into the sand. Bets looked confused, then giggled lamely at Doug, who shook his head and tossed the ball back under the net.

"COME ON!" Micki hollered, from the spread of towels and blankets and fast-food wrappers where she sat with Laurel. "Show those nerds, Bets. Show those bozos. Slam one for womankind."

Bets shrugged, looking around at the boys while Thompson posed for Micki, showing off his bicep. Then he kicked sand at Doug from under the net. Micki laughed and pretended to throw up.

"I don't know why Bets doesn't slam Thompson's brains out," Micki said to Laurel. "She could beat any of those guys, if she really tried. She's about the best athlete in our whole class. I don't know why she never tries out for the teams at school." Now Thompson was standing with his hand on his heart as if he'd just been awarded an Olympic medal. He looked over to see if Micki was watching him. Micki rolled her eyes and turned back to Laurel. "He's so predictable."

"Join the game, Micki," Thompson called when she wouldn't react to his pose. Then he clapped his hands together and his toothy grin appeared. "Just don't play on our side."

"No, thanks," Micki taunted back. "It's bad enough just watching from here."

Doug perked up and improvised a rock song called "Watching You Badly." He snapped his fingers and wiggled his hips until a wet dog who'd been roaming the beach bolted over and jumped on him.

"Whoooaaa, puppy," Doug sang.

"Love at first sight," Micki laughed.

Doug threw open his arms and tried to dance with the dog, who quickly wriggled away and trotted back to the shoreline. Soon Doug stopped dancing, Thompson stopped posing, Bets retreated to the back court, and the game began again.

Both Micki and Laurel settled into the shallow depressions they'd made for themselves in the sand. Laurel was sketching the ocean, and Micki was figuring out plans for the rest of vacation week. Micki wasn't tempted to join the game. Unlike Bets, she was a lousy athlete. Plus, the nearly all-male teams produced enough competitive macho energy for the next ten football seasons. Competition was the last thing Micki needed these days.

Especially because she was still thinking about Page. Page's spring break victory kept flashing onto Micki's brain like an announcement on an electronic scoreboard. No matter how hard Micki tried, she couldn't get her stupid thoughts to shut off. As it had turned out, most of the girls in the Class of '89 crowd had stayed in Redwood Hills for Page's vacation activities. Even the ones who were usually loyal to Micki. They'd given excuses about Bets not having room to put them up — though Bets's funny little cabin slept twelve and there were only the three of them, plus Bets's mom. But Micki knew that even the girls who supported her couldn't always resist Page's starched glamour.

Still, almost a dozen guys had shown up. They were either camping out like Doug and Thompson, or staying with Kevin down at Arch Cove. It was weird how, even though Page was gorgeous, boys seemed afraid to get too close. When they were sophomores Page had been a flirt. But since she'd been on this serious leader kick, she reminded Micki of dry ice. The kind that burns.

"What are you drawing?" Micki asked Laurel, hoping to unplug Page from her brain. "Can I see?"

"Sure." Laurel tipped her paper toward Micki. As usual, Micki was amazed by what Laurel had drawn. Instead of a blue and white ocean scene, or the contrast of Doug's Hawaiian shirt, Bets's faded sweats, and Kevin's Redwood High swim trunks, Laurel had drawn a surreal cartoon. The waves were capped with faces and outstretched arms. Micki recognized Jed. And Laurel's father.

"Laurel, that's fantastic."

Laurel looked surprised. "You think so?"

The power of Laurel's drawing really did wipe

Micki's mind clean. For a moment she just stared at it. "You are so talented."

Now Laurel seemed embarrassed. She took off her glasses to clean them on her skirt and put her pad down on the blanket. "What are you working on?"

"Me?" Micki looked down at the bright pink plastic notebook she'd been doodling in. "Oh. Organizing the week. I can't help it. You know me." Micki blew wispy hairs out of her face. "Doug wants to go clamming. Thompson says he knows all about the tide pools — but he always says he knows all about everything. I was thinking of organizing a scavenger hunt for next weekend, but there won't be enough people. Ugh. I shouldn't worry about it. It's vacation, right?"

"Right."

Micki tore out a sheet and crumpled it. "Anyway, this list can get thrown out to sea."

"What is it?"

"A shopping list Bets's mom helped us make for her spaghetti dinner. Useless. Most all the guys are going back into town for Page's party next weekend. It sounds like everyone's going."

"Not me."

"Really?" Micki sighed and dug her toes into the sand. "Actually, I might even end up going. Just to prove . . ." She looked over at Laurel, who was watching her carefully with her brilliant green eyes. "To prove that I'm not intentionally *not* going. If that makes any sense."

Laurel thought it over. "I think I understand."

"Laurel, do you ever talk to Page anymore?" Micki asked suddenly. Laurel seemed so private and reserved that she was a mystery to a chatty dynamo like Micki. And they so rarely had a chance to talk. Either they were in a group at school, or Laurel was with Jed and Micki felt like an intruder.

"Not really." Laurel picked out a new pen and went back to her drawing. Micki had a funny feeling that one of those waves was about to take on Page's perfect features. When they were freshmen, Laurel had been Page's only close friend.

"I haven't talked to Page in almost a year," Laurel admitted in a voice barely audible over the radio and the constant hoots of the boys. "It's weird. To have been best friends with someone, and then not even know them anymore."

"That is weird." Micki looked over at the game again. Bets, the strongest server in all of fifth-period gym, was letting Kevin Michaelson show her how to sock the ball. Micki thought about the ups and downs that she and Bets had gone through. At least they'd always gone through them together.

Laurel was carefully shading in seahorse-shaped sections of long, dark hair. It *was* Page appearing on the paper. "I'm right near Page's house all the time, too. Whenever I go to the vineyard to see Jed. Sometimes I even see her. I never wave or anything."

"Why?"

Laurel kept drawing. She didn't look at

Micki. "Jed feels weird about it. She lives in that big house, has a new car, and he's out in the trailer. It's the old hired-hand thing."

"Still, you could go talk to her."

"Page could walk across the field and talk to me, too."

"I just mean, you shouldn't not do anything just because of Jed." Micki stopped her mouth, sure that her words had spilled out too harshly. It was just that she couldn't imagine doing or not doing anything just for the sake of a boy.

If Laurel was offended by what Micki had said, she didn't show it. She went right on drawing.

"You know," Micki said, hoping to get off the subject of Page once and for all. "Your dad told me you aren't supposed to be seeing Jed over this week. I thought I should tell you. He sort of made me promise that you would really be with me and Bets the whole time."

Laurel's head snapped up. In a rare display of temper, she pounded her fist on the sand. That was another mysterious thing about Laurel. There always seemed to be this pool of emotion just under her skin, but Micki rarely saw it surface. "I don't believe he did that."

"He told me when I came to pick you up, when you were getting your stuff together," Micki backtracked. "He was trying to talk me into coming back early to go on that open house trip to U.C. Berkeley."

"That figures."

Micki watched the game again. Actually, if she hadn't been so hung up about Page, she'd have signed up for the Berkeley trip herself. U.C. Berkeley was the best state university in Northern California, and the following weekend was an open house for high school students. Micki just didn't want to take part in one of Page Hain's events.

"What did you tell him?"

"I told him we could just drive down to Berkeley from here. It really would be fun. We *do* all have to start thinking about college. Maybe we should go."

All of a sudden Laurel snapped her sketch pad closed. She threw her pen back into her basket and grumbled, "He thinks he can tell me what to do and run my life."

"Who?"

"My dad. Who do you think?"

Micki wasn't sure how to react. She was used to a friendship with Laurel that was polite, affectionate, and a little bit hands-off. "Laurel, he is your father."

"Micki, whose side are you on?"

"No one's." Micki stood up and pulled off her T-shirt. "I don't take sides," she insisted. That was the whole point of things now. Why she was no longer involved in school politics. Why she would even show up at Page Hain's party. She didn't take sides or stands any longer.

Laurel shook her head and her pale hair swung. "I'm not mad at you."

"I know."

"I'm sorry."

Just then the volleyball came right at Micki, with such aim and intensity that she knew it had been pitched at her on purpose. It dropped just short of her feet and was pillowed by the sand. Micki shouted, "Thompson!" and kicked it back.

"It's volleyball, not soccer, Micki," Thompson yelled.

"Who asked you, Thompson," Micki mumbled to herself. Predictably bad timing, pain-in-the-rear Thompson.

Laurel was looking up at her, clearly regretful for having taken whatever frustration she had with her father out on Micki. "It has nothing to do with you, Micki. Really. I'm sorry."

"Forget it."

Thompson was still yelling. "Well, Michelle, are you afraid of all these superintelligent men, or are you going to play?"

"Spare me." Micki patted Laurel's shoulder and said, "See you in a little bit. I need to take a walk or something."

Laurel nodded.

Micki began to run, her calves working hard across the dry sand. When she approached the game, Thompson started in on her again, but she ignored him and kept on going.

Doug hummed the theme from *Rocky* and mimed playing his saxophone, but Micki ignored him, too. She wasn't getting into any game where there was a score, a team, sides and serves and setups and slams. She ran faster, enjoying the wet air against her face, and thinking what a sensible idea it was to take a slow, solo jog.

* * *

"Um, where's Micki going?" Bets asked Doug as she watched her best friend getting smaller and smaller along the shoreline. She knew that Micki wasn't overly fond of exercise and only ran when she felt like her figure absolutely depended on it. Why, when Bets needed her, would Micki decide to do such an unpleasurable thing?

"I don't know," Doug said. He flicked back his hair and got in position for Thompson's next serve. "Bets, cover the back court, okay?"

"Oh, right. Yeah. Sure." Bets moved back. She couldn't figure out why Doug was so irritated with her. She wasn't showing him up, making him feel inferior or anything like that. But it didn't seem to make any difference. No matter how she tried to make Doug treat her the way he used to treat her, it just didn't work. In fact, recently she sensed that everything she did just got on his nerves.

"This is it. Point and match," said Thompson. He jumped dramatically, then pounded the ball over the net.

The ball popped back and forth. Bets was far away. She was vaguely aware of Doug's blond hair, which was the color of a collie's fur, as opposed to Kevin's swimmer's blond, which was more like stalks of bleached hay. She thought about how Doug was so talented in music, plus smart and funny. No wonder he had outgrown her — just like L.P. had. Everyone in the junior class was talented or smart and funny or something.

Betsy Frank was the only person in the entire

Class of '89 who didn't have a thing going for herself. Not grades or some great college waiting. Not some adoring boyfriend or special talent. She supposed that she was okay-looking and her parents weren't poor, although they were certainly far from rich. But she could barely get a word out without getting tongue-tied and when she did get the words out, they never seemed to mean what she wanted to say. Maybe Micki could keep up with boys like Thompson and Doug, but not her.

"BETTTSS!"

Bets was so busy thinking that she didn't hear Doug's warning or even see the volleyball slanting down like a missile past her face. Kevin Michaelson dove in front of her with his arms outstretched. He was just wearing his Redwood swim trunks and his shoulders were starting to peel.

"Mine!" Kevin called, managing to flip the volley back. After he tipped the ball, he tumbled into Bets, and she tried to catch him, her arms wrapping around his slim, bare V-shaped chest. She felt his warm skin, the scratch of his dry hair. He fell, pulling her down with him, and she suddenly realized that Kevin was one boy who didn't seem annoyed with her. He'd been smiling at her all through the game.

"ALL RIGHT!" Kevin yelled, holding on to Bets a lot longer than he had to.

Even though only Kevin's arm was touching her, Bets seemed to sense every part of Kevin — from the smell of his hair to the calloused parts of his toes. It was amazing. She felt like she had never been this close to anyone before. Stretched out on the soft sand with him she felt safe and warm like a little kid. On the other hand, they weren't little kids, and both of them knew it. Bets tried to get up, especially when she noticed that Doug was frowning down at them. But Kevin's hands circled more tightly around her waist. "Hey, Bets," he said in her ear in the funniest way.

Bets wasn't sure what to think for a second. She didn't know Kevin very well. He was one of those popular boys who usually paid attention to the beautiful girls like Page or Cindy White. All she knew was that somebody was finally noticing her and that he didn't seem to blame her for not returning the volley. Bets leaned into him and giggled. "Um, hi."

Finally they got up and he was staring at her with sleepy brown eyes. She stood awkwardly while he brushed the sand from her knees. Not sure what she was supposed to do, she giggled and brushed the sand from his knees. He laughed.

Bets had a fleeting feeling that something was going on here that she didn't quite understand and might not really be interested in pursuing.

But when Kevin said, "Hey, Bets. Maybe I'll drop by your house one night. We can walk on the beach," she nodded and said, "Oh. Okay."

If Doug wasn't going to pay attention to her, and Micki was going to run away, then Kevin Michaelson just might have to do.

CHAPTER 5

On Monday evening, Micki was in top form again. She'd jogged for three days in a row, learned how to body surf, and was enjoying the beginning of a perfectly even tan. Each day the morning fog had lifted, the weather had been great for swimming and volleyball, and then the nights were cool and breezy.

"I'm telling you, Doug. There's no more clamming here," Micki insisted.

They were sitting on the sandy living room carpet of Bets's cabin. The room was low-ceilinged and decorated with seashells and fishing nets. Instead of couches, there were two single beds with bolsters under the windows. None of the furniture matched, and all through the house there was the rolling, distant sound of the ocean.

Nobody responded to Micki's announcement. Instead, Thompson crouched over the playing board like a hawk. He wiggled a finger at Doug. "Roll the dice. It's your turn."

Doug, wearing a straw hat, a suit jacket, shorts, and no shirt, scooped the dice off the game board. Then he stood up, wagged his hips, stomped the floor, mumbled a few nonsense words. Finally he blew on the dice and threw.

"Whoa, whoa, whoa," he yelled out.

Micki sighed. It was typical Doug game behavior and he, along with Micki and Laurel, was challenging Bets, Thompson, and Kevin Michaelson in a game of Trivial Pursuit.

"Oh, no!" Kevin cried when the dice turned up five dots and Doug smugly slid his marker to a Geography square. Doug's team needed Geography points to win, and Doug was surprisingly good at it.

Kevin moaned again and threw himself into Bets's lap. One way or another he'd been throwing, bumping, knocking, and leaning himself into Bets all evening. Micki thought she hadn't seen so many collisions since she'd watched the National Highway Safety Commission movies in Driver's Ed. Bets giggled, but Micki didn't think it was funny. To keep from thinking about how unfunny it was, she brought up the subject of clam digging again. "Dougo, what do you really think is going on with the clams?"

Doug waited anxiously for his card, motioning for Micki to give him a break and leave him alone. Patiently she waited, while he answered the Geography question — wrong, it turned out. He scowled, then did little whimpering noises when he looked back over at Micki. "Sorry," he said.

"No biggie, but I wish you would tell the truth about no more clamming."

"What do you mean, no more clamming?" Doug asked, waiting for Thompson to pick a question card. He tilted the straw hat over his eyes.

"There aren't any more clams, Doug," Laurel surprised Micki by answering. "Micki, Bets, and I found out."

Doug had told them all about clams. How he used to dig for them in the sand. How they looked like tiny, prehistoric creatures in the steamer pot. How they tasted better than french fries or the Bubble Café's onion rings.

"How can there be no more clams here? When I was a kid we used to come out here and get bushels full every time we went digging." He demonstrated with his hands, then widened the picture. "I'm talking major bushels!"

Laurel's green eyes took on an unusual twinkle. "Maybe *that's* why there are no more clams here."

Everyone laughed. Laurel was usually so quiet, or so attached to Jed that it seemed like she was behind a screen. Over the last few days, Micki had noticed Laurel opening up . . . coming out of herself. Laurel had been a little like this last spring break, but that was when she was just getting together with Jed, before that relationship seemed quite so all-consuming. Now Micki hoped that Laurel was coming back, but she was worried that she might not because of Jed.

It wasn't that Micki didn't like him. How could she not like him; she didn't really even *know* him. Nobody did, except Laurel. When Micki saw him it was always like meeting him again for the first time. Always that awkward and always that shy. She never knew quite what to say, and he acted like he didn't want to say anything. It was frustrating for Micki, since she was so used to bringing even the shyest people out. Maybe that's why she considered it a kind of personal defeat.

But more worrisome was the fact that Laurel seemed to be willing to do anything to be with Jed. For instance, Jed was expected to sneak over that night. In spite of the promise Micki had given Laurel's father, Jed was on his way. It didn't seem to matter to Laurel that Micki had stuck her neck out by telling her dad that there was no way that Jed would be around while they were at the beach. That fact seemed to go right past Laurel. She would do anything to be with him, and it didn't matter who got in the way — her father, her friends . . . anybody.

In the face of Laurel's passion for her boy-friend, Micki didn't quite know what to do. She wasn't even sure she could relate to how Laurel was feeling. There had only been a few times when Micki had been that excited — when she had led class meetings, or organized the home-coming parade as a freshman, or presented a social studies project. She couldn't imagine get-ting that wired just over a boy, but then, Micki hadn't had much experience with boys. What little she did have — like her crush on Jason Sandy freshman year — had turned out to be pretty dismal.

At that point there was a hollow knock on the screen door that opened out to the droopy back porch of the beach house. Micki didn't even have to look to know who it was. Jed was there, behind the tiny checkered pattern of the wire screen. Laurel jumped up to invite him in.

"Hi."

"Hi."

All of them turned. Doug waved at Jed. Thompson nodded. Bets gave a big smile and Micki simply looked.

Jed immediately started backing further out of the light — almost as if he were going to disappear right off the porch. "Want to come in?" Laurel said brightly.

"I thought we'd go down the beach," Jed said in a low voice.

Laurel didn't offer any resistance. She quickly went over to the couch to pick up her old beat-up denim jacket with the corduroy collar and slip on a pair of sandals. "We'll be back later," she said, leaving things open-ended.

Everybody joined in a collective good-bye. Laurel and Jed slipped out. A moment later Micki heard the rumble of Jed's motorbike.

"Unfair competition now," Thompson teased. "Two against three."

"I can still show you, Thompson," Micki bragged. She picked up the question cards and shuffled them.

"You don't have to count me," Bets mumbled.

"Bets," objected Micki.

"I just, um, mean, I never know any of the answers." She ruffled her short hair and looked embarrassed.

Kevin nudged Bets with his foot again and stood up. "Yeah. The game's not fair now." He gave Bets a heavy-lidded smile, reached out his hand, and pulled her up. "Let's go walk on the beach."

Bets didn't say yes, but she didn't say no. She merely let Kevin tug her toward the door, Micki observed, just like she'd let him paw her all evening.

Micki reached for her parka. "Maybe we'll all go," she said.

But it was too late. The screen door had already clacked shut again. For a moment Micki, Doug, and Thompson sat uncomfortably.

Finally Thompson picked up the dice and shook them. "Okay, you two. Let's start over. I'll take you both on."

This time Doug wasn't picking up Thompson's cues. He wasn't interested in their usual two-man joke routines. Instead he scooted onto one of the twin beds that sat under the window. He lifted the curtains, which were trimmed with fuzzy blue pompoms, and peeked out.

Micki and Thompson watched Doug. After a moment, Doug let the curtain down and slumped back on the bed. His clean-cut features were creased with concern. Micki was always amazed at the thoughtfulness and intelligence in Doug's blue eyes in those rare moments where he wasn't joking or cutting up.

"You look worried, Mr. Markannan," Thompson said in a corny voice. "What's outside that window?" Thompson divided the deck of cards in half and mimed a chomping mouth. "Jaws?"

Doug tried to smile.

"Orca the killer whale?"

"All those clams you murdered when you were a kid?"

"*Dawn of the Living Dead* clams?"

"You two are such dorks. Come on," Micki said, grabbing the cards and collecting the plastic markers. "Let's play. The three of us individually. The winner gets to read the U.C. Berkeley catalogue out loud in the car, when we drive down to U.C. Berkeley for that open house."

"The losers have to listen," said Thompson. He plugged up his nose and twanged, "Class number 493 in Earth Studies. Our moldy earth — or why earthworms make your garden better."

"Thompson!"

They both noticed Doug lifting the curtain and peeking out again.

At the same time, Micki and Thompson bounded over to look, too. What was out there? Most likely, the other guys were surrounding the house, stringing the fence with toilet paper. Bets's mom — who was out that evening delivering baked goods to an elderly lady in Arch Cape — would love that.

Micki lifted a corner of the old curtain and stuck her face up to the glass. Right away she saw what Doug was looking at. The only thing to see out there in the tiny front yard besides Doug's Cadillac, were a couple of bicycles chained to the picket fence, a mailbox, and Bets and Kevin. But Bets and Kevin were making out like crazy — like a couple who'd known each other for ages. Micki had been to parties where couples would suddenly be wrapped around one another at midnight. They were people who (from what Micki could tell) barely knew each other. Now that she thought about it, Micki realized that Kevin Michaelson was sometimes the guy part of those couples.

Micki violently turned back around. She was terrifically embarrassed. "Doug, you pervert."

"I'm going to go," Doug said, his face now turning a burning red. He dropped the curtain. "I want to get up early tomorrow. I think I'm going back to town."

"Back to town?" Thompson exclaimed. "But it's only Monday. We still have all week of vacation."

"Are you coming back?" Micki asked.

"I don't know."

"What about the open house? This weekend at Berkeley."

Doug shrugged. "Can you take care of the camp fire without me?"

Thompson made caveman grunts and nodded. Doug left without another word. "Just you and me, Micki," Thompson said.

"Oh, goodie." Micki smirked back. She resisted the impulse to lift the curtain to watch Doug leave, and turned her attention back to Thompson. For a fleeting moment, Thompson dropped his smugness. His face relaxed, and for the first time Micki noticed a seriousness behind that Tom Sawyer face.

Micki wanted to ask him, Why are my friends doing these things? Why is Laurel sneaking off with Jed, when her dad made me promise she wouldn't? Why is Bets out there necking with Kevin Michaelson, when he probably isn't really interested in her? And why did Doug pick the third day of vacation to suddenly bail out and go back home? Something inside her sensed that Thompson might be asking himself a few of those same questions. Or even that he might know one or two answers.

But instead of mentioning her concerns, she flipped over the card. "I bet you know what country a true Bohemian lives in," Micki said.

The thoughtfulness fled and the cocky smile returned. "Czechoslovakia."

Micki slapped down the card as he pushed a wedge into his plastic wheel. "Thompson," she said, "you are so predictable."

CHAPTER 6

Things change.

Driving back to Redwood Hills the next morning, Doug kept thinking about how things change. He could start with his dad's old Cadillac. When Doug was tiny, this car had seemed the height of luxury and elegance. Now it was a white elephant of a gas guzzler that Doug's sixty-five-year-old father preferred not to drive.

Doug patted the dashboard. "No offense, old guy," he told the car, "but you're a dinosaur. An endangered species, like those poor old clams." He cruised on, turning off the two-lane coast highway, and heading onto the curvy wooded road that led back home.

Doug settled into the thick, springy seat and turned on the radio. He flipped stations, just as interested in the news and the talk radio as the rock and jazz. That had changed, too. Doug still loved music, but he was interested in tons of other things now, too. War novels and geography. Movies, computers, and outer space. How to make a rock video and what made people act the way they did.

There was something else that had changed. Doug used to be a joke. But he didn't feel that way about himself anymore. Sure, he still made jokes. He still liked jokes. He just didn't have to joke all the time or pretend that something was a big laugh when deep down it really bugged him.

Maybe that was why this thing with Bets bothered him so much! It had partly to do with changing, and partly to do with what made people act the way they did. When they were underclassmen, Doug had been wild about Bets. He didn't care that she wasn't flashy or fast. Actually, that was what he'd liked best about her. She seemed so secure in just being sweet-tempered, brave-hearted Bets. Doug might even have loved her.

He still loved her. Just not that way anymore. Junior year he'd realized that it was okay to be weird Doug Markannan. That had really hit him last fall, during their big band competition. Everyone had wanted to do a musical theater medley, or John Phillips Sousa, or some equally predictable entry. Doug insisted on Charlie Parker tunes. He'd even helped Mr. Weeden, the band teacher, with the arrangement. He followed his weird instincts, and they'd won.

Maybe that was what bothered him about Bets lately. That she didn't have a sense of taking who she was and running with it. She was hanging back, waiting for other people to show her that she was okay. It really bugged him that she couldn't see through a guy like Kevin Michaelson. Maybe Doug was wrong. Maybe Kevin really cared about Bets. Maybe the way Kevin had previously gone after only the most popular girls, and then bragged that all the rest were putty in his hands was a thing of the past. Maybe Kevin had changed, too. Doug hoped so.

"Hooooomme," Doug chanted in an E.T. voice, half singing with the radio, half relieved to see the gentle rolling hills that made his hometown such a good place to cultivate wine grapes. It was even warmer here than it had been at the beach. As Doug pulled into downtown, he stuck his head out the window, let his blond hair flutter and sang, "Home, home for spring break. Where the deer . . ."

"Doug-o!" answered a loud voice from somewhere on Main Street.

It was Paul O'Conner, waving his baseball cap, standing in the parking lot of the World For Women Health Club, a gawdy warehouse-type building that housed a female-only spa that appealed mainly to old ladies. A draped Venus statue stood in front — the brunt of many a joke in Redwood Hills. Micki always wanted to petition for a matching male statue in front of the hardware store.

Doug steered the huge car across three lanes and pulled into the entrance. "What's up, O'Conner? Did they finally make you a member here?"

Paul, who was tall and stocky with a preference for hockey and coveralls, rolled his eyes. "Ha. ha. It's that CPR and first-aid class that Page organized. They're refinishing the gym floor at school, so it got moved here. Cindy White's father owns this place."

Doug slipped on his sunglasses and took in the site. Cindy was a good-looking bleached blond who'd been voted "junior most likely to die from exposure to a sun lamp."

"That figures," Doug said.

"Yeah."

"So what are you doing out here? Why aren't you inside, saving the world from heart attacks?"

"I'm going, I'm going." Paul looked over at the big World For Women sign and cringed. "I'm just taking my time about it. Hey, I thought you were camping at the beach." He punched Doug's arm. "Too many mosquitoes?"

"Yeah, sure." Doug didn't want to discuss the fact that he wasn't sticking around to watch Kevin and Bets. "Hey Paul, I'll go to this CPR thing, too. Wait for me." He stepped on the gas and called back, "I'll keep those old ladies from calling you names."

Doug drove away too fast to hear Paul's reply, which he figured was not worth hearing. He quickly parked, thinking more and more that spending the afternoon reviewing CPR was probably a good idea. He hadn't gone over it since taking a first-aid class last summer, and it was one of those things that everybody should know.

He and Paul tramped in together. As soon as they stepped through the double doors, Doug felt almost as awkward as Paul. Everything was decorated in lavenders and pinks and smelled like moldy powder. There were more statues, and notices about facials and cellulite. Doug felt more uncomfortable than if they'd accidentally walked into the girls' locker room.

"Where are we supposed to go?" Doug asked.

Paul pushed him toward a desk in the lobby. Not a big metal table, like they'd have at the Y, but a thin-legged, antique desk decorated with gold paint. Page Hain was sitting behind it. She wore a sweatsuit so white it could have been in a bleach commercial. Her long hair was loose, although Doug had the fleeting impression that she looked like a nurse. An incredibly gorgeous nurse.

"Hi, Page," Paul said in that polite, hands-off way that boys seemed to treat Page with this year.

Page had a smile that looked like she was ordering her mouth to curl up. It didn't strike Doug as having much to do with feeling good inside. "Hi, Paul." She checked Paul's name off her list. "Go on in. We're about to start."

Paul, who was usually pretty gruff, nodded politely and headed toward what looked like the main gym.

Doug hung back. He'd never really understood why boys acted as if Page Hain was a piece of see-through china. He didn't know her very well — his friendship with Micki automatically put him and Page on opposing sides. Until debate this semester, Doug hadn't been in a class with her. Still, Doug remembered when he and Page had posed as Bam-Bam and Pebbles Flintstone for their freshman homecoming float. The girl who'd goofily paraded in front of the entire school dressed in a cavegirl outfit with a dinosaur bone in her hair didn't seem to fit with the starched, uptight beauty at that antique desk.

The thought of that homecoming float so filled Doug's mind that he grinned and said, "Yo, Pebbles."

Page, who was collecting her things, froze. She hadn't acknowledged Doug so far, even though it was impossible for her not to have noticed him. "Excuse me?"

"You're excused."

"Did you say something?"

"Who, me?" Now Doug knew why boys were so stand-offish. The air around him felt like it had dropped ten degrees. Doug shifted, tugged on his sweatshirt — which said, THIS IS A SWEATSHIRT, and repeated, "Yo. Pebbles."

Page's milky skin reddened as if someone had spread paint just under the surface. She looked around, making sure that no one else had heard him, then became very busy, moving pencils, neatening the desktop, checking the names on her list. "Your name isn't on the sign-up list."

"Really?"

"Yes."

"I knew that."

The class was starting inside the gym. A woman, who sounded tough and authoritative, was telling everyone to sit in a semicircle on the floor. Page picked up her clipboard and went over to the gym doorway.

Doug followed. "It's okay for me to come, isn't it? You wouldn't want somebody to croak just because I didn't remember how to save them, would you?" He knew he was being obnoxious, but something about Page's rigid lack of humor egged him on.

"No," she snapped. "I wouldn't." They both stayed in the doorway, waiting for a polite moment to enter. The gym was pink, too. Pink carpet. Pink exercise equipment. Most of the equipment had been shoved to the sides of the room. In its place there were several life-sized plastic dummies, some charts, and the instructor, who was introducing herself as Mrs. Zucker of the Redwood Hills Fire Department.

Page stayed in the doorway, going over her list again and counting heads.

"Is everyone here?" Doug whispered.

"Why don't you just go on in and listen."

"I'm listening. I've had this before. I just came for a touch-up. Spur of the moment." He bumped her with his shoulder. "I'm a spur-of-the-moment kind of guy."

"I'm sure you are." Page was obviously so eager to get away from him that she no longer waited for a pause in Mrs. Zucker's speech. She marched in, stepping over her adoring classmates and the plastic practice dolls, finally taking a seat in the opposite corner.

Doug sat near the door. The instruction began, but Doug found himself still watching Page.

She sat barbell straight, moving only occasionally to smile at the other juniors: the Dubrosky twins or Carlos Oneda or her other admirers. Doug was fascinated by her smile. It wasn't phony — actually Doug didn't think anything about Page was really phony, despite what Micki said. Her smile just didn't sit right on her face. For some reason he remembered the smile she'd worn in the parade as a freshman. That was a smile she couldn't help wearing, as opposed to one she had forcibly stuck on.

Mrs. Zucker was beginning with mouth-to-mouth resuscitation. She called it "artificial breathing" and that term drew Doug's attention back to Page. Page did artificial smiling, he decided. She was so different from someone like Micki — whose smile reflected her interest in the entire world. Or Bets, whose non-smile exposed exactly how unsure she felt inside.

"Everyone line up so you can try it for yourselves," Mrs. Zucker said at the end of her demonstration. She gestured for them to stand and try out their new skills on the practice dolls.

Doug realized that he was practically missing this entire lesson, and made himself review it in his head as he got in line. For some reason the dummy was named "Annie" — just like in first-aid class. First, check and see if "Annie" is only asleep — you didn't want to start pounding away if someone wasn't in distress. Open the airway. Find the pulse. Press the sternum down one and a half to two inches. Alternate breathing with pumping. Fifteen compressions per two breaths.

By the time Doug had gone over the whole thing a few times, it was his turn. He knelt next to "Annie," asked if she was only sleeping, opened the airway, tested, and checked. Then he carefully placed his hands and pushed. Strong and rhythmic. Mrs. Zucker nodded for him to keep going. It was hard work.

"Perfect!" Mrs. Zucker finally cried enthusiastically. "Did you all see that? This young man was the first one to really get it right."

"Thanks," Doug said, looking up and feeling relieved that he'd learned something, in spite of how distracted he was. After all, with his elderly parents, he had to take this class more seriously than most of his classmates.

He moved away to let Cindy White practice next. As he backed up he almost stumbled over someone's foot and then reached out to balance himself. Then he felt a switch of thick hair against his cheek and something inside him panicked. He was already a little winded from doing CPR, but now his heart was flipping like the rotor on a helicopter. He'd run into Page.

"Sorry," he blurted.

"What?" she asked.

"I bumped into you. I . . . nothing. Forget it."

Page barely looked at him and he went speechless. Him! Doug Markannan! Page had succeeded. She'd intimidated him, cooled him out, just like she'd done with every other boy in the junior class. Doug was furious with himself. That was not the way Doug Markannan faced life! But he didn't know how to remedy things now, and so he turned and started to walk away.

"Don't go," Mrs. Zucker said suddenly, holding her hand out to stop him.

"Me?"

She nodded. "Once everyone has had a chance, I want a couple of you to try it as a pair."

"Okay." Doug came back and there was Page's barbell-straight back again. Right in front of him, waiting to take her turn after Cindy.

That's when his brain did the weirdest Doug Markannan weird thing. He had this crazy flash all of a sudden that Mrs. Zucker was going to ask him to demonstrate mouth-to-mouth resuscitation on Page. In front of everyone! The thought embarrassed him so completely, that he made stupid, chuckling noises and shook his head. He couldn't get the ridiculous thought to go away.

"Will you stop laughing!" Page demanded, not looking at him. She sounded like a teacher.

"Sorry." He tried thinking about "Annie," his algebra midterm, the answers to all the Geography questions in Trivial Pursuit. Why in the world had this idea about Page even occurred to him? He was still chuckling, although the laughter didn't feel like it was really coming from him. "Really. I had this very weird thought. I get them a lot."

"I don't doubt that."

"A very weird thought," he repeated.

Page ignored him.

"Actually, I was thinking about giving you mouth-to-mouth resuscitation."

That got her attention. She whipped around, whapping his chin with her hair. "WHAT!"

"Next," said Mrs. Zucker.

Page looked around her as if she was searching for an escape route. But it was her turn to practice. She dropped down next to the doll and began pumping. But she was still so stunned — or angry — that she first forgot to lift Annie's head back or check a pulse, and then began pumping in the wrong place.

"Hold it!" Mrs. Zucker ordered. She pointed to Doug. "You did it so well. Come back and show Page how."

Page's eyes got wider, as if she really did think she was going to have to lie down in front of everyone and have crazy Doug give her mouth-to-mouth.

"Guide her hands," Mrs. Zucker clarified.

Page looked only slightly less alarmed as Doug crouched beside her. He rested his hands on top of hers.

Page's fingers tensed. "Let's just get this over with," she pleaded in a smoky, hushed voice.

"Annie, are you okay, Annie?" Doug asked, leaning his head over Page and shaking the doll's arm. "Are you just asleep?"

Page's jaw clenched.

"I don't hear any snores." He knew he was making stupid jokes, but there was no going back now. He was so aware of her tense hands under his, the nearness of her shoulder and the lilac smell of her hair. Wow! This was almost as good as being in a field of wildflowers, Doug flashed. Except there was a person attached to this experience, so it was happening on a lot of different levels. He tried to keep from flipping out and revealing how much sensory overload he was experiencing. Coolly, calmly, but all the while oh-so-aware of trying to keep it together, Doug nudged her. "Aw, Pebbles, what if Annie is just taking a snooze and we go break twelve of her ribs?"

"Would you stop calling me Pebbles!"

"Sorry." Doug leaned over to prop the doll's head back and feel the pulse. Then he shouted in the dummie's ear, "Annie! Don't worry. Pebbles and I are here."

Page tried to slip her hands away, but Doug caught them. They were ice-box cold and as tense as two pieces of cement. So Doug swept one of Page's hands off the dummy and vigorously rubbed it with his other palm. "Brrr. We've got to warm you up, Pebbles. You're going to freeze poor Annie to death."

He looked over at her with his usual crazy grin, but suddenly everything stopped. Page didn't draw her hand back. Her eyes had filled with tears and looked like stones covered with fresh rain. Doug's stomach plummeted. He had gone way too far. He had only meant to make her smile — really smile. To get through that hard exterior. He'd had no idea that he was really upsetting her, or that she could be hurt that easily. He felt like a bigger jerk than Kevin Michaelson.

Not sure what else to do, Doug held Page's hands and pressed again and again on the poor plastic dummy. He noticed a tear slide down Page's cheek, and then she covered her face with her long hair so he couldn't see anything.

Finally Mrs. Zucker told them they were finished, and Doug helped Page up. He refused to let go of her hand, even though she tried to pull away. He was trying with all his heart to get a silent message to her by way of his grip. I didn't mean to make you cry. I actually admire you and would like to find out who you really are.

Page stood next to him, her hair still guarding her perfect features. Finally she flung her hair away and gave him a look that at first felt like a slap, and then seemed like a plea.

Doug didn't know what to make of her. But for the first time, he really wanted to find out.

CHAPTER
7

A Frisbee sailed above the shoreline. It dipped. It dove. Like a tiny red spaceship with a mind of its own, it suddenly shot away from the sand and flew out over the surf.

"Fake out, fake out," Micki teased Laurel. "Give it up."

Laurel was having too good a time to give up. Even though she was wearing rolled-up pants and one of Jed's paint-stained shirts, she ran into the ocean. Knees high, she splashed and tasted saltwater and shivered. The disk was within arm's reach and she lunged for it. "Ahhhhh!"

"Grab it," Micki encouraged.

A wave of water whapped at Laurel's legs. She was down. Water rushed over her head. Wet clothes swirled around her and for a moment the world was the most wonderful pattern of grainy green decorated with streams of brown seaweed. Then the waves shot her back up again. She was still holding the Frisbee. She felt victorious. "Look!"

"Yay! Success!" Micki thrust her fist into the air. "Too bad those dumb boys aren't around to see that."

Laurel threw the Frisbee back to Micki, as intensely as if she'd been hurling a discus. Micki caught it.

"Race you to the blanket," Laurel challenged.

Micki crouched. "Ready, set, go!" She took off.

Splashing wildly, Laurel made her way out of the water. She wasn't a very fast runner, but Micki was even slower. They made it up to the blanket at exactly the same time.

Bets was waiting for them, sitting alone, slapping together some sandwiches. When they flopped down on the blanket she raised her hands, as if the two pieces of white bread she held would keep her from getting wet. "Don't, um, drip all over the potato chips."

"Sorry," Micki replied. She shook her hair like a wet dog. Bets cringed. Usually Bets didn't care if she got wet, dirty, covered with thistles, or dragged through the mud. "Bets, how come you didn't go in the water?"

Bets shrugged.

"Oh, that felt great," Laurel sighed, groping first for a towel, then for her glasses. "I have to remember the way it looks when you're under water."

"Did you really see stuff?"

Laurel giggled. "Sure, Bets. I saw seahorses down there, and something orange and blobby that pulsed." She mimed a beating heart with her delicate hands. "Maybe it was a jellyfish."

"Really?"

Micki affectionately knocked against Bets. "And I saw the Loch Ness monster."

Bets deflated. "Oh. I get it."

"We're kidding."

"I know."

Laurel reached for her sketch pad, then realized that she had to wait until her hair and clothes weren't quite so drippy. She sat cross-legged, closed her eyes, and let the sun rest on her cheekbones. She tried to imprint that swirly underwater pattern on the inside of her eyelids, so that she could go back to it when she was ready to put it on paper. Meanwhile, she imagined things that could be decorated with a design like that. Wrapping paper. Floor tiles. Notebook covers. Fabric and stockings and sunglass frames.

Micki was drying her legs. "Any sign of the guys yet?" Kevin and Thompson were meeting them. They planned to explore the tide pools down in Arch Cove.

Bets stared down the beach. For the first time that afternoon, she smiled. "No. Net yet. Do you think Doug really left?"

"I'm sure of it. When Doug-o makes up his mind to do something, he usually does it."

"Well, um, why? What's he going to do back home?"

"Nothing probably." Micki pulled on a turquoise T-shirt over her bikini top and the old satiny boxing shorts that had belonged to her brother Peter. "He'll practice his saxophone. Mope around. Miss us." Micki giggled. "Have a terrible time."

"You think so?" Bets rubbed her eyes. "I still can't figure out why he left."

"Don't try. You know Doug."

"I guess. Oh, Kevin said he'd come for us about one."

Micki checked her watch. "Good. We have some time before he and Thompson get here." She grabbed her backpack and foraged through it. There were Career Day pamphlets in there, plus postcards, glitter socks, a half dozen college catalogues and a handful of Day-Glo barrettes. Finally, she pulled out a small paperback with a photo of a sea anemone on the cover. It was titled *Life in the Tide Pools*. "I bought this book when I went into town yesterday. If smartface Thompson tries to act like he knows everything, I'll beat him to the punch."

"I hope they're not late," Bets worried.

"Don't worry. Thompson is always disgustingly on time." Micki stretched out her arms, which were turning almost the same pecan color as her hair. "Who cares anyway. We'll have trouble getting rid of them. I don't even mind anymore that Doug left. It's more fun with just the three of us." She opened the book and looked at drawings of starfish.

Bets handed each of them a sandwich.

"Thanks." Laurel took a big bite. "It has been fun, hasn't it?" She gave Bets a reassuring pat.

For Laurel, this was starting to feel like a real vacation. A change. A breather. Not that she'd ever admit it to her father, but she was glad she hadn't stayed home.

The first night she'd had that awful, empty ache of missing Jed — just as she'd expected. It was a feeling that was scary and hollow, like staring endlessly at a blank page and fearing that no picture would come to her. That's how she always felt at those endless weekends with her mother. With her mom, she'd learned to sit back from everything, so that time could pass without touching her. She'd nod when her mother babbled on about the new baby, or when her stepfather lectured her about how bad Laurel's vegetarian diet was for her health. Laurel would pretend that they were actors in a foreign movie. She'd watch their mouths and scramble their words until she heard nothing but noise.

But over the last few days with Micki and Bets, Laurel never remembered to scramble their words. She was too interested in what they were saying, or else she was right in the middle of things and to scramble the conversation then would have been to scramble herself. She didn't have to worry about staring at a blank sketch pad, either. Her brain never seized up. The pictures kept on coming.

"Maybe I should study oceanography," Micki said, chomping her sandwich, still reading the tide pool book and opening the Berkeley catalogue. It was amazing how many things Micki could do at the same time.

"Is that like fish and stuff?" said Bets. "Ew."

Micki nodded and happily kicked her feet on the sand. "Laurel, are you going with us this weekend? We're definitely going to that open house thing at Berkeley. We'll organize our own little trip from here. Only sunburned people allowed."

"Doug, too?" Bets said hopefully.

"I doubt it. Nerdy Thompson is driving, though. We talked about it last night after he beat me twice in Trivial Pursuit. After you two deserted me," Micki said pointedly. Both Bets and Laurel looked a little sheepish. "Anyway," Micki giggled and pointed her nose in the air. "We get to ride in his mother's Mercedes."

"Okay," Bets said unenthusiastically.

"You have to go," Micki reminded Laurel. "Whether you like it or not. I promised your father. Remember."

Laurel shook her head. "I still don't believe my dad did that to you. All my dad cares about is that I don't spend every minute with Jed."

"Laurel, maybe it's none of my business, but is Jed going to keep coming out here? I know I shouldn't care, but I did promise your dad. I don't like lying to people."

"My dad is being ridiculous."

Suddenly a *beep-beep-beep* poked into Laurel's thoughts. Good. She wanted to tune out Micki and the others right now. She didn't want to discuss Jed or anything personal. An electronic beep, in fact, was about as personal as she wanted to get.

"Ten to," Micki reminded her. It was her watch alarm that had just gone off. "Laurel, you told me to tell you when it was ten to."

"Time to call, um, your dad?" Bets asked.

"Not my dad. Jed."

"Jed?" Micki put a hand to her mouth as if she hadn't meant to say it in such an appalled tone of voice. She looked at Laurel and saw that her friend was absolutely expressionless. Okay, Micki thought, I blew it. She tried to smile, then she spread out her catalogues in case Laurel wanted to take a look. She was devouring the one from U.C. Berkeley.

"I guess I can wait a few minutes," Laurel stalled. "I don't have to walk up there this second."

Just for this once, Laurel wished that Micki wasn't quite so quick and perceptive. She wasn't dragging her feet about calling Jed, she told herself. She'd just gotten an idea for a drawing and, since Thompson and Kevin were due to arrive any minute, she wanted time to jot it down.

Still, there was this new feeling she'd been experiencing lately that was the opposite of the hollow loneliness she felt away from Jed. This was more like being in a very crowded space, like the San Francisco buses at rush hour. It was a place that she had to map out very carefully. My foot goes there; my elbow there; my secret thoughts over there.

She'd had glimpses of this feeling before last night, but that was when it really hit her. At first she'd been so happy to see Jed again that there was nothing but total lightness and the beautiful picture of his face. But somehow, as soon as they'd left the cabin and the others, it seemed so quiet. His motorbike rumbled and they heard the roar of the ocean when they stopped to walk on the pier. But then Laurel told Jed about the new ideas she was having for her drawings, the long swims, and the jokes during games of Trivial Pursuit.

"Trivial is the word for it, all right," Jed had scoffed. Then his shoulders tensed and he was in that moody place where there was no getting through to him. He didn't want to dream about what they'd do when they were on their own. He didn't even want to kiss her.

By the end they'd had a little fight. She worried about him driving all that way home at night on the bike. He'd argued back that he wouldn't need to drive all the way out here if she hadn't come to the beach. She said it was her dad that made her come and Jed looked at her with those inky blue eyes that said that he knew the sound of an excuse, even though it happened to be true. So she'd promised to call him today, and every day. At exactly one o'clock.

"There's Thompson!" Bets cried hopefully. She touched her hair and tugged on her shorts, arranging herself for the arrival of the boys.

They waited as Thompson climbed over the small hill that separated the beach from the highway. Thompson hiked, he waved, he stood out against the white bluff in his red windbreaker and golf hat. He didn't hurry. He didn't look back. He was alone.

Bets's smile vanished and her strong body sagged.

Micki picked up Bets's concern right away. "Kevin's probably meeting us from somewhere else." She laughed. "He probably didn't want to spend the morning with Thompson."

Bets perked up a little. "Probably."

It took forever for Thompson to saunter across the sand and reach them. He grinned first at Micki, then at the other two girls. A smattering of freckles had appeared on his cheeks. "Hello, ladies." He took off his hat and bowed cornily. While he was bent over, he noticed Micki's open tide pool book. "Ah," he teased, "studying the elusive hermit crab."

"I only wish that you would hide in your shell, Thompson. Where's Kevin?" She asked it off-handedly. She could tell that Bets was dying to know, but that she didn't want to be the one to bring it up.

Thompson dug a hole in the sand with his deck shoe. Now he wouldn't look at Micki. Micki suddenly realized that it was totally out of character for him to be evasive. "Well, he can't make it, actually." Thompson looked at Bets and smiled. It wasn't his usual smart-aleck grin, but a smile that reflected sympathy and a desire not to make a big deal out of this. "He said he's really sorry."

Bets pulled her legs in and rested her cheek on her knees, as if she was trying to make herself as tiny as possible.

"Why? What happened?" Micki blurted out.

"Well," Thompson stalled. He glanced back up at the bluffs, as though if he could stall long enough, then Kevin would actually appear. "See, his mom made him go into town and get stuff for the house."

"Oh, well, that explains it." Micki realized that she was acting almost as unnatural as Thompson.

Laurel seemed uncomfortable, too.

"Can you wait about fifteen minutes, Thompson?" Laurel asked. "I have to go make a phone call."

Relieved, Thompson folded onto the sand next to Micki. "I can wait forever."

Micki rolled her eyes. "Spare me."

Bets suddenly pulled off her sweatshirt and started running along the sand. "Then I'm going for a swim."

Micki watched her from the back. Bets's short hair fell perfectly. Now that Micki thought about it, she realized that Bets had spent about a half hour in the bathroom this morning getting her hair right. Even though Bets was pretty in a wholesome, farm-girl way, she didn't usually wear makeup or fuss with her looks. Today she was wearing lipstick and eye shadow. Plus, Bets usually would have been the first one in the water. She would have disappeared over the horizon and appeared again a half hour later, barely winded. Today she hadn't gone in the water at all because she wanted to look extra pretty for Kevin. Kevin, who hadn't bothered to show up.

"Well, Thompson Gaines the third," Micki said, "it's you and me again."

Thompson lay back on one elbow and

squinted at the sun. "I know," he grinned. "Can you stand it?"

"Probably not. If I ask you a serious question, can you give me one serious answer, Thompson?"

"I think we're too young to get serious, Micki."

"Thompson!"

He grinned.

"Kevin didn't really have to do errands for his mom, did he?"

"Really? You mean really, like in reality really?"

"No, I mean pretend really." Micki buried her face in her hands. "I should know better than to discuss anything important with you."

"In reality, Kevin went body surfing with Greg and Sam Pond and three girls they met on the beach this morning."

Micki felt almost as betrayed as Bets. "He didn't tell you to say he was sorry, did he?"

Thompson shielded his eyes from the ocean glare and shrugged.

"He didn't care that Bets was waiting for him."

"Some guys are like that."

"What a creep."

"A 'creep'?" Thompson repeated, making fun of the word.

"You think what he did is okay?"

"I don't think that at all. I just wouldn't refer to him as a 'creep.' "

"You wouldn't?"

"Unadulterated slime is more like it."

"Thompson, don't make jokes about it. It's not funny."

"I'm not joking. I don't even like Kevin. Or respect him."

"You don't?"

"Of course not. How can you respect a guy who treats girls like that?"

"I don't know."

Thompson shrugged. "Me, either."

"Well, why not?" Micki tossed back, suddenly off-balance and not sure what else to say. "You're the one who's supposed to know everything."

"You finally admitted it."

Micki found herself staring at him.

"What are you looking at?" he asked, glancing around.

"Who, me?" Micki had the strangest, most unsettling feeling in her limbs, as if her blood had been replaced with sparkling water. She took a deep breath. "Nothing. Nothing at all."

CHAPTER 8

Page sat cross-legged on her white canopied bed. Her bedroom was on the second floor and the windows were wide open. Beyond the fluttering lace curtains, she could see for acres. Past the trailer where Jed lived with his uncle. Past where the dirt road connected to the highway. All the way to where the rounded mountains fitted with the sky.

It was bright out there today. So bright that the green looked almost yellow. Dry, gusty, and hot, too. The kind of day that was standard for August or the first week back at school. Usually spring break had in-between weather that drove Page crazy with longing for summer. Or sometimes it was downright gloomy and cold. A frustrating throwback to frigid December. As cold as . . . Page Hain.

"Pay attention to what you're doing," Page scolded herself, trying not to think about Doug and what he'd said to her during the CPR class. She went back to the papers spread out before her and focused on the bus list for the U.C. Berkeley trip, which was taking place that Friday.

Page didn't know why she was dignifying Doug's remarks by giving them a second thought. She didn't know why Doug had gotten to her so thoroughly. Every time she thought about him — which was about every five minutes since the CPR class — her fists tightened and her heart would pound. Boys like Doug didn't matter! Page told herself. They only had influence if you allowed them to have influence. They only spoke the truth if you believed it to be so.

Besides, Doug was Micki Greene's good friend. No matter how carefree Micki acted, Page never believed that Micki'd forgiven her for taking over her position as class president. How could she? Page saw the way Micki watched her in debate class, how Micki grinned with self-satisfaction when she presented a persuasive argument. Her grin said, Take that, Page Hain. You may be the big class big-shot now. Other kids may think you're Jeanne Kirkpatrick or Sally Ride. Not me. I know you're as lame as Miss Redwood Hills Grape Harvest.

"Ugggghhh," Page groaned, willing herself to concentrate. She had to call everyone and tell them what time they were leaving, then Xerox U.C. Berkeley maps and information sheets. She was relieved to have so many busy, orderly tasks ahead of her. Anything was better than thinking about Micki. And Doug.

She set out her list of phone numbers. But before she could reach for her princess phone, she heard a tentative knock on the bedroom door.

Whitney stuck in her fluffy head. "Page, do you mind if I come in?" she asked in a dusky, baby-doll voice.

Page became immediately suspicious. When she was a freshman, Whitney had bossed and humiliated her. Sophomore year, Whitney had convinced Page that she had to make her mark in her class, no matter who she hurt in the process. Page used to think that Whitney just didn't want to be embarrassed by the way her little sister had turned out. Now she worried that all Whitney really wanted was to have Page under her control.

"I have a lot of things to do," Page said firmly. "Do you need something?"

"I was just thinking about you." Whitney pouted and wound a piece of dark, silky hair around her finger. Page never ceased to be amazed at the gooey, seductive act her sister put on — not only with boys, but with teachers, other girls, even their parents. The disgusting thing was that it usually worked. Page was about the only person who saw through it, and she'd only been able to do that for the last year.

"What about me, Whitney?"

Whitney strolled in. A can of diet soda appeared from behind her back. She presented it to Page. "It's getting so hot out. So I brought you this."

Page nodded and took the can.

"I thought you'd want it."

"Whitney, thanks for the soda. If there's something you want, tell me. Otherwise, I have things to do."

"I was just thinking about this party you're throwing," Whitney huffed. "You've been so busy with all your stuff this week, I thought you might need some help." She plopped down on the edge of Page's bed. "Excuse me for worrying about my little sister."

Page put aside her lists and phone book. When Whitney acted like this, she had to pay attention and be on her guard. "I thought you hated my class. Last week you were furious with me because I left you alone in the living room with my friends."

"I know," Whitney cooed. "I was awful, wasn't I? I was in such a bad mood. It seems like my class just wants to graduate and get things over with. They barely do anything together anymore. Maybe I was just jealous."

Page wondered if jealousy *did* have something to do with Whitney's hot and cold way of treating her. Last year Whitney'd accused Page of retreating into nothingness. But perhaps Whitney hadn't intended for Page to become quite so powerful. Page's accomplishments now made Whitney look like the nothing.

"Anyway," Whitney sighed, "I know how much work it is planning a big party, and I wanted to offer my help."

Page popped open the Diet Pepsi. "Thanks. But it's not going to be any big deal. Mom and

I are buying a ton of chips and soda on Saturday morning. Dad already asked some of the workmen to clear out the back of the tasting room." The tasting room was a big, chalet-shaped building where tourists could taste Hain wines. There was an area in back for banquets and parties. "I'll set up my stereo and people will bring records. That's all. So really, there's not that much to do."

"That's all? Are you serious?"

"Yes." Page wasn't really comfortable with her family's wealth. She'd decided that the party would be casual and simple, despite the expectations of some of her classmates. "It's all under control."

"You're so organized," Whitney whined. "I would be running around like a crazy person. You don't even need me anymore."

"Whitney, you're my sister. Of course I need you."

"No, you don't. You have everything going for you now."

"Whitney."

Page was incredibly grateful to hear the phone ring. She didn't think she could stomach having to coax Whitney out of a sulk. She turned away, hoping that Whitney would pick up the cue and leave her alone. But no. Without hesitating, Whitney lunged across her and took the receiver. Page pushed down her annoyance. She and Whitney each had private phone numbers. The call had to be for her.

"Hello," Whitney answered in a smoky purr. A second later she thrust the receiver away from her ear as if the other party were screaming. Page heard scraps of music coming out of the telephone. A jazzy wail, played on a single instrument.

"Who is this?" Whitney demanded, in a much less appealing tone.

"Who is it?" Page whispered.

"Hello. HELLO!" The music stopped, and Whitney put the phone back to her ear. "This isn't Page, this is Whitney. Will you tell me who this is?" Her painted nails rapped impatiently on the antique telephone table.

Suddenly the recognition of that musical instrument zapped Page from her fingers to her toes. A saxophone! There was only one person — one boy — who would be crazy enough to play his saxophone over the telephone before even saying hello. Ooh, what was he calling for? To remind her that she was too cold to touch a 'plastic dummy? To rub it in that she was a hard, inhuman iceberg? Page's entire body felt like it had been jolted by lightning, and she flew across the bed to grab the phone out of her sister's hand.

"Page!" Whitney objected, stunned by Page's impulsiveness.

As soon as Page had the phone, she realized that she had done a very stupid thing. She was not the kind of person to fly or grab. Careful not to expose the way her heart was throbbing and her hands shook, she put the phone to her ear. It was like riding a roller coaster, while pretending she was sitting on a park bench.

"Page? It's Doug Markannan."

Whitney was staring. Page wasn't sure why, but it was essential that she hide Doug's identity. Maybe it was because Whitney had thought that Doug was the height of geekdom way back on that freshman float. Maybe it was because Page felt as vulnerable as a freshman right now, and she didn't dare expose herself to her sister.

"Page, this is you, isn't it?" Doug's voice no longer had that cocky ring to it.

"Yes," Page finally managed.

"Who is it?" Whitney growled.

Page put her hand over the mouthpiece. "Just someone from my class." She cleared her throat and went back to the phone. "Can I help you?"

"Can you help me?" Doug laughed. "That's a good question. I think I need help. Don't you?"

"Excuse me?"

"No need for excuses. Maybe it's not help I need. Not exactly. See, the way I figure it, it was mostly my fault. Not that you don't act royally stuck-up sometimes. You do. But I know I'm kind of a clown. That's okay. I can live with that."

Page was making herself stay calm. Meanwhile her heart was smacking her ribs so hard, she thought she'd fall over. Just then Whitney stole her bus list and wrote *WHO?* across it. She shoved it in Page's face. At the same time Doug was rambling on, making some kind of joke that Page couldn't follow.

"Yes. I see," Page replied stiffly into the phone.

"You see? Really? I see that the basic reason

I called is to say that I'm sorry for bugging you so much. I was a jerk. I went too far. I never meant to make you cry."

"You didn't." Page wanted to say that it wasn't him that had made her cry. It was her contact lens, a sudden memory of her dog's death. Of course, she didn't wear contacts, and her dog was still alive. But she didn't want him to know how he had hurt her.

She said nothing, because Whitney was yapping at her, too. "I'm telling you Page, you have gotten carried away with this whole leadership thing. I don't know who that is on the phone, but you can't be involved in everything. You don't even have the time to plan a decent party."

"It doesn't matter," Page snapped at her sister.

"Do you really think that?" responded Doug. "Great! If you feel that way, I agree. It doesn't matter at all."

"Not you!" Page cried.

Whitney looked outraged. "What do you mean, not me? I give great parties. I'm known for giving the best parties in my entire class."

Page felt like she was going insane.

"Anyway," Doug continued, "since you feel that way, I have this weird idea. I know you'll think it's weird, but I'm a weird kind of guy and maybe you're weird, too, underneath all that nonweirdness."

Page sat paralyzed, afraid to say anything.

"So how about if you and I go out tomorrow night?"

"What did you say?" Page gasped.

Whitney answered her. "I said, you can ask anyone in the Class of '88 about how great my parties. . . ."

"I know it's radical," Doug laughed, "but we'll do something radical and it'll be great. So, what do you think?"

"Page!" Whitney was railing, "I know you're on the phone, but you could at least pay attention to me. Do you want me to leave you alone or something?"

"YES!" Page exploded, burying her fist in her mountain of pillows. "YES!"

"YO!" Doug rallied in response. "All right! I'll pick you up at seven. It'll be an experience. Great. See you then. 'Bye."

Click.

Then there was nothing but a dial tone and Whitney's silent sulking. Page put down the receiver. Her blood was crashing through her veins. She felt like she was going to faint.

"I thought you at least liked me," Whitney grumbled after a few minutes.

"What?"

"I am your sister. I never thought you'd yell at me like that to leave you alone."

"I'm sorry."

"No, you're not."

"I was on the phone."

"You weren't talking to anyone important. It was just some dumb kid in your class reporting about that college trip or some lecture. You weren't even saying anything."

Page collapsed back into the lace pillows and the stuffed animals. She was seeing stars. "The other person was saying something. I was listening. Or I should have been listening. Did you ever think of that?"

"Oh, yeah?" Whitney sat up and took a healthy swig of the Diet Pepsi. "So who was it?"

Page closed her eyes. She was swirling and sinking. Swaying and feeling a little sick.

"Exactly." Whitney's bow mouth stretched into a triumphant smile. "What did I tell you?" She finished the soda, got up, and marched to the door. In the doorway, she turned back. "So do you want me to help with your party?"

"What?"

"Your party Saturday night. I'll help. Maybe I'll invite a few college people. There are two girls from Julianne's sorority that I need to have over."

Page barely heard her.

"Okay?"

"Oh. Sure."

"Good." Whitney gave her an angelic look, spun around adorably, and at last, was gone.

Page stared in front of her. She was shell-shocked. Completely stunned. No matter how strongly she willed her life to proceed in an orderly fashion . . . the world was still a very crazy place.

CHAPTER 9

"Not over there! Set them up along the wall.
Along the wall, Walker! Is that a wall?"

"No," Jed mumbled belligerently. "It's not a
stupid wall."

"Well, then don't put the boxes there."

Jed locked eyes with the Hain Winery foreman, a balding, block-shaped man named Roy.
It was Wednesday and they were in the banquet
area of the tasting room, clearing things out for
Page's party. Jed wanted to tell the foreman that
if he set the wine crates against the stupid wall
they would just have to move them again when
they did business during the rest of the week.
But did anyone listen to him? Of course not.

Roy was still glaring. So Jed picked up a stack
of crates and deliberately let them down hard,
so that there was a loud thud and the dull tinkle
of glass. Jed wiped sweat from his face. It wasn't

nearly as warm as yesterday. Instead it was drizzling and the air was heavy.

Roy pointed a finger and scowled. "You," he spat out. "If you really want to work for me, you'd better change your attitude real fast."

Jed knew Roy was asking for a "yes, sir." But he wasn't going to get it. Maybe Roy thought getting hired for weekends and summers was the greatest thing that had ever happened to Jed Walker. Maybe he thought that Jed would get down on his hands and knees to keep this one-day-old job. If Roy did think any of those things, he knew even less than Jed thought he did.

Jed had sworn from the time he was in eighth grade that he would never take a real job on this vineyard. Not since he got in a fight at school after some boys had written "hired hand" on his books. Oh, sure, he'd helped his uncle for an hour here or there painting fences or clearing brush. But that was only pickup work, doing a few of his uncle's jobs in exchange for what other kids called allowance. This was different. This job had a punch card and schedule, an hourly wage, and a boss. He'd taken it because it was the easiest job for him to get. He'd decided to buy something with the money he'd make . . . something important. But now he wasn't sure if he could stick it out long enough to earn the money.

"Let's move it, Walker," Roy prodded. "When you're done with those boxes, bag up the trash in the back and set it out for pickup."

Jed nodded mutely. He didn't mind hard work. He had just wanted his first real job to be away from this place. Away from all of Redwood Hills. Somewhere where they would value his skills at fixing motorbikes and machines, where they'd think he was doing okay with his junk sculptures. Where he wouldn't feel humiliated to have Laurel — or anyone else — see him working there.

This all went back to Laurel. She drew her surreal cartoons and imaginative designs, but she could also draw a realistic picture of a vase of flowers or a building or a car. They used to talk about how that kind of literal art was dull, highly inferior to his sculptures, which were abstract shapes made out of discarded pieces of metal and wood. But lately, Laurel became quiet when he insisted that illustration and commercial art were for non-talents. And that made him suspect that his junk sculptures were exactly that: pieces of junk.

Jed continued to stack and carry . . . and think about Laurel. He knew that she was dreaming of a world outside Redwood Hills. Not a fantasy world like the one he looked forward to, but a real one with colleges and art schools and other people. That was another reason he needed money right now. Not just spending cash, but real money that would allow him to keep up with Laurel, no matter where she decided to go.

"Hey," the foreman yelled, bursting into Jed's thoughts. "Finish with those boxes and bag that stuff out back. What are you thinking about? Necking with your little girlfriend?" He laughed. A dirty laugh that turned Jed's stomach. "Get going!"

"That's just what I'm about to do," Jed spat back. He knocked over a stack of folding chairs and, as they clattered to the floor, walked out into the rain.

It was raining out at Ocean City, too. The air had grown so thick that the sky was a spongy sheet of gray. The surf went wild. By afternoon the beaches were almost deserted, leaving only a few dogs and the most dedicated joggers. Everyone else had stayed inside. It was the kind of day for baking nut breads and reading books.

That's about how Micki, Laurel, and Bets had spent their time. Bets also helped her mom hang new curtains, while Laurel worked on her underwater drawing, and Micki memorized the answers for fifty question cards of Trivial Pursuit. They all enjoyed the rest. Still, when Thompson stopped by unexpectedly, explaining that he was on his way to a movie, they didn't hesitate to grab their slickers and go.

"And you thought there wouldn't be a crowd for the seven o'clock show," Micki taunted when they arrived at Bayside Cinema. The ticket holders' line stretched past the Haystack Bakery and the Ocean City Video Parlor. The air smelled of cinnamon rolls and was punctuated by the bings and boings of Donkey Kong. "Thompson, why do I ever listen to you?"

"I didn't know you did listen to me, Micki. But now that I do know, I'll take advantage of it." Thompson rattled the change in his pockets and winked. The way he humored Micki made

Bets think of the world's most patient baby-sitter.

"That's what you think, Thompson the third." Micki smirked. "That is, when you *do* think."

"Do I think? I don't know. What do you think?"

Bets was getting worn down by their constant banter. Junior year was hard enough without trying to keep up with them. "What if Jed comes down?" she softly asked Laurel, turning away from Micki and Thompson. "He won't know where you are."

Laurel pushed her glasses up her nose and craned her neck, as if she really expected Jed to appear. "He won't be here. He said something about working all day and tomorrow on the vineyard. The phone call was kind of strange. He hates working there. I wish he was coming here tonight."

"Yeah."

"It seems like such a long time until I see him again on Saturday."

"It's just a few days."

"I know," Laurel said. "It's just too long."

Laurel seemed worried or uneasy, but Bets wasn't sure how to comfort her. She'd felt closer to Laurel over the last few days, but it still seemed as if Laurel was from a slightly different planet — a girl who knew what it was like to really be loved by a boy. Very different from boring Bets. Not sure what else to say to Laurel, Bets examined the crowd. There were enough tanned teenagers to dot the beaches from Santa Cruz to Bodega Bay.

"Are you looking for somebody, Bets?" Micki wanted to know.

Bets knocked her cowboy boots together and shrugged. She realized that she was looking for Kevin. She still hadn't seen him since the night they made out in front of her cabin. She'd invented a hundred reasons for his absence. Kevin had been grounded. Sent home. Taken ill. Maybe his swim coach had called and told him to practice laps fourteen hours a day. Anything made more sense than the painful thought that he had been crazy about her one night, and then forgotten her the very next day. "Um, I thought maybe Doug might come back."

"Is he coming back?" Laurel turned to Thompson. "Thompson, have you talked to Doug?"

"I had to call him from the highway pay phone last night."

"Why?"

Thompson gave Micki a you're-going-to-love-this-one look. "I couldn't remember how to set up the tent."

"What did I tell you?" Micki gloated.

"Well, why didn't you just go stay at Kevin's?" asked Bets.

For the first time Bets could remember, Thompson didn't reply right away. For a split second he looked as tongue-tied as she felt most of the time. But whatever had stalled him, passed quickly. A second later his Tom Sawyer grin was back and he was jabbing Micki with his elbow. "I said I was going to rough it this vacation, so I decided to rough it. I always make good on my word."

Micki busted up. "What did you do? Sleep in a half-pitched tent in the rain?"

"I am many things, but I am not stupid. I slept in the Mercedes."

Micki howled.

"So, well, um, what did Doug say?"

"Yeah, what did Doug-o say?" Micki giggled, barely recovered. "Should we wait for him on Friday before we drive down to Berkeley? Is he coming back?"

"I don't think so," Thompson said. "He said he was glad he'd gone back home, because there had been an interesting development."

"What does that mean?"

"It means, Bets," Micki interrupted, "that he had to go get his teeth cleaned."

"No, um really," Bets repeated. "What development?"

"I don't know," Thompson grinned. "There was a huge bug in the phone booth, and by the time I got rid of it, I'd run out of quarters."

Micki guffawed. "An ant, probably."

While Micki and Thompson went on teasing each other, Bets mumbled, "Never mind." She was glad that the line was starting to move. They were waiting to see *Some Kind of Wonderful* and Bets stared at the movie posters as if she could climb into them. Being in a big dark room with nothing more to think about than a story up on screen was exactly what she wanted right now. The line chugged forward to where they could smell popcorn and no longer hear PacMan.

They were a few hundred feet from the door when three male voices cried at the same time, "THOMPSON!!"

Bets spun around and saw Kevin with seniors Greg Kendall and Sam Pond. All three of them were racing over from the box office, stuffing their money and tickets in their pockets and waving wildly. Bets gasped with hope. Kevin was grinning, his big, jock's smile lighting up his peeling face. Her hand lifted into the air and she smiled, too, until the boys arrived and gathered around Thompson. Kevin didn't even look at her. Not even a glance. Bets felt like she was loaded with bricks again. Tons and tons of them. Slowly, she lowered her hand, pretending that she had only raised it to neaten her hair.

"Thanks for saving us a place, guy!" panted Kevin, slapping Thompson on the back.

"Actually, I didn't." Thompson sounded surprisingly cool. He let them cut in, but then crossed his arms over his madras shirt, stuck his nose in the air and said not another word. For once, Micki was quiet, too.

Bets was jostled ahead of Laurel and found herself staring at the back of Kevin's head. Short hair, overbleached from chlorine. Sunburned neck. Redwood letterjacket dribbled with drops of rain. They moved ahead in an even pace toward the door, and she felt as if a conversation were taking place between her and the back of that head.

I'm here. Remember me, she was pleading si-

lently. Someone notice me. Please just turn around and say hello. Tell me you don't hate me and that I haven't done something terribly wrong.

But that head kept right on going, seeming to respond, *You don't matter. I don't even see you, but if I did I wouldn't really care.*

When they finally reached the ticket-taker, Kevin turned around. He looked past Bets, as if he was searching for someone else. "Hey, Bets. How's it going?" he said quickly. Then his ticket was taken and he was gone. He didn't even wait for her to say hello back.

Bets handed over her ticket. By the time she stepped into the lobby she felt wobbly and confused and was holding back tears. Plus, she'd lost Micki and Laurel. There was a big, busy crowd, all rushing to get to the candy counter. Bets let herself be pushed back, almost into the drinking fountain. She decided that if she could just make it into the theater, she would find Micki. Micki would have a seat saved for her. Micki always did. Micki would be kneeling on a chair, waving and making such a scene that Bets would find her no matter how crowded it was.

Then someone touched Bets's arm. She breathed in buttery popcorn and her tears almost burst onto her cheeks.

"Micki?" She almost sobbed.

It wasn't Micki. It was Greg Kendall. Greg was a Redwood senior with dark, close-cropped hair and a right-angle jawline that reminded Bets of Superman. Greg usually hung out with his own Class of '88. All Bets really knew about him was that he was Sam Pond's best friend, that he was staying at Kevin's house, and that he was the only one to have started vacation with a tan. His face was even browner now, but she could still see the old outline of ski goggles.

"Hi, Bets," Greg smiled and leaned against the wall next to her. He tossed popcorn in his mouth, then held the carton out for Bets.

Bets didn't take any. Seeing Kevin had made her mouth feel like dust and her stomach like quicksand. For some reason Greg's smile just made her feel like she was losing even more ground. She was sure that if she tried to eat popcorn, she'd choke. "Uh, did you see where everybody went?"

Greg stood on tiptoes and searched. He was about the same height as Bets and wore a striped ski sweater with white jeans. "Nope." He was shooting kernels into his mouth now, as if he were a little nervous. "I hear this movie's great."

"Oh."

"Yeah. It's supposed to be very romantic." Greg sort of smiled to himself, then nudged her with his shoulder.

"Are you sure, um, you don't see Micki and Thompson?"

Greg looked again, then checked his watch. "No, I don't see them. We'd better go sit down, though. It's starting." He held his hand out to Bets and gave her this odd expression. Eyebrows raised. Eyelids lowered. "Come on. Let's sit upstairs. Just you and me."

The music swelled from inside the theater.

Bets figured that it was only the coming attractions, but nonetheless when Greg tugged on her arm, she felt as if there was no time left and she had to take any seat she could find. She went up the stairs with him.

When they reached the top he said, "We'll find everybody afterward."

Bets stole a brief glance over the balcony before Greg led her back. She *did* see Micki sitting next to an empty seat, which she was saving with her rain slicker. Micki squirmed and searched until the man sitting behind pointed his finger and lectured. Then Bets didn't see anymore because she was moving to the back with Greg.

The upstairs was darker than the first floor, but Bets could see a little as they groped for a seat. There were a lot of couples up there. *Some Kind of Wonderful* was just beginning, but most of the kids up here didn't seem to care. It was pretty embarrassing to hear the giggles and smacks and see the arms wound around necks and shoulders. This was the make-out zone. Greg led her down a row of empty seats and they sat down.

Bets tried to look relaxed as Greg's arm slipped around her. In reality she was nervous and unsure. She didn't know what to do with her hands. She watched the blonde girl on the screen, a girl about her age, playing her guts out on a set of drums. Bets's heart was suddenly flailing as wildly as those drumsticks. She shifted, shoving Greg's arm away.

They watched the movie for a few minutes, but soon Greg leaned over and whispered, "Aw, come on, Bets." He stared at her. When she didn't move, he lifted the side of her hair and began to kiss her earlobe and her neck.

Bets closed her eyes. She was starting to feel warm and woozy — the way she used to feel with L.P., and with Kevin. This wasn't as strong as the feeling she'd had the one time that Doug had kissed her. But in some ways, this was better. Easier. With Doug it had been too scary, too breathtaking, too much like falling off a mountain or floating through the air. Nonetheless this was a lovely, exciting feeling; one that chased all that heavy bricked-up doubt right out of her head.

Finally Bets turned her head and let Greg kiss her mouth. As soon as she did, his other arm encircled her and he pulled her so tightly to him that the armrest dug into her hip. She put her arms around his neck, and the movie faded away as they kissed again and again and again.

CHAPTER 10

Doug kept his eyes on the road. Even though the rain had let up, the freeway was still steamy, and the lights were stretched out of shape. Off ramps flipped by. He hummed along with his Wynton Marsalis tape, tapped the steering wheel, and tried to remember why a date with Page Hain had ever seemed like a good idea.

"We're almost there."

No response.

"You okay?" he rambled. "Are you cold?" Page cringed noticeably and Doug wanted to stuff his mouth full of old socks. "I didn't mean . . . I just thought you might want the heater on."

"I'm fine."

"Fine. Good. I'm fine, too."

She was sitting so far away from him that Doug thought of asking if she preferred the backseat. She clutched her jacket. She stared out the window. In her pale gray shirt and slacks, she reminded Doug of a paratrooper about to take a terrifying jump.

Doug cleared his throat. "Not too much longer." He tried to sound confident. When he'd thought up this date idea he'd been convinced it was original and brilliant. But now that he was forty minutes into the drive and barely a word had been uttered, he was beginning to wish that he had simply taken Page to the Bubble Café for a Coke and an order of fries.

"There goes Vacaville," he announced, feeling like a demented tour guide. They were traveling south, on their way to Marin County.

Nothing.

"Good old Vacaville. You know what Vacaville means? No? Well, it means Town of Cows. Makes you kind of glad you live in Redwood Hills. Doesn't it?"

Zip.

"Oookay."

He drove a while longer listening to Wynton's trumpet and the conversation inside his own head. He almost launched into a dozen opening lines. Why did you wait for me halfway down your driveway, instead of making me bumble through "Nice to meet you Mrs. Hain," and "I'll have her home by midnight, sir,"? Gee, Page, are you always such a barrel of laughs? Aren't you interested in where we're going? Maybe I'm taking you to Alcatraz . . . ha ha. Or, Page, why in the world did you agree to this date when you obviously can't stand me? It was weird, that's what it was. Doug still couldn't quite believe it was happening.

Whatever the case, he couldn't take this much longer. Maybe Page was intent on having a terrible time, but not him. He'd expended a fair amount of money and energy getting tonight's tickets on such late notice. He'd vacuumed the car, used spray starch on his Frank Zappa T-shirt, stopped by Nordstrom's cosmetic counter and dabbed on some Calvin Klein cologne. The more he thought about how great it would be to really get to know Page, the more jazzed he'd become. And now? Now he wasn't getting to know anyone — except maybe Wynton Marsalis. This was like spending an evening with a block of cement.

When it was almost time to leave the freeway, Doug turned off the tape player. Instead of Wynton's quartet, Page was going to get solo Doug.

"Gee, Doug," he said out loud, "you sure are taking me a long way just for a date."

He turned his head and, lowering his voice, answered his own statement. "Well, Page, to tell you the truth, this isn't just any date. I'm pretty intrigued by you. I know you don't like being teased about Pebbles and the float when we were just weird freshmen, but I know that I'm still weird underneath this cool, Robert Redford exterior. And I wondered if maybe you were still weird under your cool, Robert Redford exterior, too?"

Page actually shifted against her seat belt. She pushed back her hair so that Doug could see one of her gray eyes. He couldn't tell whether she was finally looking at him because she was amused, or because she thought he was insane. Whatever, it was a first step.

They swerved down the Sir Francis Drake Street exit. He kept mouthing off. "I'm just trying to break the ice . . ." She cringed again, which made him cringe, too.

"No insult intended." He reminded himself not to mention another word referring to temperatures below seventy degrees. "We're going to the San Rafael Coliseum. Now maybe I should have asked you what you felt like doing, but I don't think we're doing too well in the communication department, so I took it upon myself. I'm a take-things-upon-myself kind of guy."

He stopped at a light and glanced over. She was really looking at him now. He seldom saw her eyes so clearly. The intelligence and the determination he saw there were impressive. Such direct contact made the wisecracks fly out of his head.

"Sorry I'm being such a clown," he heard himself say in a much softer voice, "but if you agree to go out on a date, you could at least talk to me."

She began twisting the strap of her shoulder bag so intently that he thought it would snap. "Sorry."

"Don't be sorry."

"Well, what do you want?"

"I don't want anything. Except to have a good time. I thought that was the whole point of dates. Not to torture each other."

"I wouldn't know," she said with difficulty.

"I don't go on very many dates."

Doug was aware of his dopey, caught-off-guard expression. Since Page was so beautiful, he'd assumed she had a date every weekend. That was one of the reasons he'd asked her out the way he did. He figured if he tried anything resembling a normal approach, she would turn him down. On the other hand, he didn't know anyone who had dated her. And when he saw her at school events this year, she was always there in her official capacity. By herself. "Why not?"

"Why not what?"

"Why don't you go out on lots of dates?"

He thought he might have gone too far again, but after a moment, she answered in a straightforward voice, "No one asks me."

"Are you serious?"

"You're the joker. Not me."

Cars started honking, and Doug realized that the light had turned green. "I am, aren't I." He turned and screamed out the window, "All right! Don't honk your brains out! I'm going, I'm going."

They drove the mile to the Coliseum in silence again. But Doug decided that he was making progress — possibly not in the right direction, but at least it was something. They cruised by the fancy shops and gourmet groceries of downtown San Rafael, past palm trees and parks and pink Spanish-style office buildings.

"You're right. I am a joker," he said boldly. "Want to hear some really bad ones?"

She didn't answer. Doug steered the car into

a wide, busy parking busy lot and waited for the attendant to show him where to park. After he'd switched off the motor, he faced her. "Okay. How many freshmen does it take to screw in a light bulb?"

Page stared straight ahead.

"The whole class. One person to hold the light bulb, and the rest of them to turn the room."

Page's mouth jiggled a little.

Doug forged ahead. "How many sophomores does it take to screw in a light bulb?"

She shrugged.

"The whole class. One to put in the light bulb, and the rest to tell her they can do it better."

"Why do I have the feeling that junior comes next?"

"Wrong! I believe in the unexpected. Instead of juniors, how many Page Hains does it take to screw in a light bulb?" Before she could answer, he quipped, "That's not funny."

She looked puzzled.

"Don't you get it? 'That's not funny' is the punch line. Since you would take the whole thing very seriously."

Page's shoulders began to tremble. Her back was heaving slightly and she had her hands cupped over her face. Doug's heart sank through the floorboards. He was a moron! An insensitive fool. He'd made her cry again. He didn't deserve to go out on a date with a girl like Page.

"Page, I'm kidding. It's a joke. I'm sorry."

But then he heard a funny sound that stumped him. It was halfway between a badly fingered note on his saxophone and the squawking of those seagulls over Arch Cove. Was she sobbing? Gasping for breath? Cursing him in some exotic tongue?

Suddenly it hit him. She was laughing! Or rather, she was trying not to laugh, but the sound was coming out despite her efforts. And because she was working so hard to hold back her laughter, it sounded all stilted and squashed.

As soon as Page realized that he was watching her, she drew her breath in and straightened up. A moment later her smile was gone and she sat with her hands folded, looking out at the rows of cars, pretending that none of this was really happening.

"I saw that," Doug teased with amazement. "Don't laugh. No laughing allowed on this date. This is supposed to be the worst night of your life."

"Don't remind me."

"Well, at least you're honest. Don't worry, it'll be over soon."

"Promise?" She gave him a funny look. A look that was kind of goofy with her mouth half open and her nose wrinkled up. Boy, he liked that look. But a moment later the look was gone and she was pulled together again. "You are as weird as people say you are," she said.

"That's me."

"Where are we?" she asked, looking out at the crowded parking lot.

"The Coliseum in San Rafael."

"Of course. You told me that."

"Hey, you really were listening."

"What are we going to see here?"

"Something great."

"What?"

"Guess."

He thought she would clam up again, but obviously she was getting curious. She watched the passing crowd. "A concert?"

"Nope."

"A ball game?"

"Wrong again."

"Holiday on Ice?" She caught her own mention of frigid temperatures and made that funny face again. But she didn't cringe. "Well, what?"

Doug did a drum roll on the dash. "Pro wrestling."

By the time the main event rolled around, Page felt as woozy and off balance as Tony the Tough Guy or Courageous Carl. It was as if she were in one of Laurel's cartoons. In the ring were huge men calling themselves Werewolf Willie and Bernie the Beast. There'd even been a match between two women — Glorious Gloria and Shauna the She-Devil. They wore costumes of fur and tinsel and their acts were more like Las Vegas stunts than the wrestling matches Page had seen at Redwood High. Something about it kept making her think of their old Flintstones homecoming float.

"Do you go to these a lot?" Page asked Doug in one of the rare semi-quiet moments.

"All the time. I think it's what I want to do when I grow up."

"That's . . . nice."

"Page, I'm kidding."

"Of course you are." Page knew that he was probably kidding. But she was so totally flummoxed by this time, that if Doug had told her that he was going to jump out of cakes for the rest of his life, she would have considered the possibility that he was telling the truth. She wasn't taking anything on this date for granted.

"What do you want to do when you grow up?" he asked her. "Do you know?"

Again, Page wasn't sure how to answer. Boys never asked her about herself. Just like they never touched her, or challenged her, or even made passes at her anymore. She didn't know if that was because they were afraid of her, or because they just weren't interested. "I'm not really sure yet. Probably a lawyer. What about you?"

"You mean, after my wrestling career as Demented Doug?"

She couldn't help smiling. "Yes. After that."

"Something to do with music probably. Maybe not playing, but something. I'm trying to figure it out. Why a lawyer?"

"I want a job where I can really use my brains."

Doug nodded.

"Why music?"

Doug thought for a moment. "I want a job where I can really use my heart."

"Oh." Page tried to think of something else to say, but Doug's reply was echoing inside her head. She sat there like an idiot, reverberating, and gazing into his soft blue eyes. She worried that there was a silly, vacant expression on her face, but she had the most unsettling sensation. Something was getting in the way of the messages she usually willed her brain to send to the rest of her body. Messages like . . . don't giggle. Don't appear whimsical or dumb. And for heaven's sake, don't make a fool of yourself. All her circuits were being jammed by some kind of strange electrical field. Her will had been temporarily stopped up. Overloaded by lightness and an odd buzzy glow.

She was grateful to Doug when he broke the moment by clapping his hands and gesturing toward the ring. "Here we go. The main event."

Page had barely caught her breath when the announcer introduced the final wrestlers. Dutch Savage and Magnificent Maurice. The theatrics began before the wrestlers even hit the ring. Walking down the aisle to make his entrance, Dutch began pounding his chest and bellowing, as if his savageness was too wild to be confined to the ring.

Doug laughed. "I love it when they do this. It's so corny."

Dutch began running like a beast released from the zoo. He had blond Prince Valiant hair surrounding a scowling face, carried a club, and wore a Viking helmet. There were shrieks as he ran through the audience swinging his club and grunting. He even picked up a couple of women until they screamed their heads off, at which point he set them down.

"What's he doing?" Page gasped.

Doug was rooting Dutch on. He leaned into Page. "It's all part of the show."

Page knew that it was part of the show, and yet something inside her was still shocked at the outrageousness. The silliness. She became even more stunned when Dutch stormed over to their section of seats. Now that he was closer she could see that his blond hair was an obvious wig, that he wore makeup and had a tattoo on his biceps that said, OMAHA. She was trying to figure out how some man from Nebraska had ended up as Dutch Savage when she realized that Dutch had his eye on her. Dutch grinned, a drooling, Neanderthal grin. Instantly, Page looked away, hoping he would swing his club at someone else.

But it was no use. Dutch was zoning in on her! Suddenly all Page could think of was when she was a freshman and an upperclass yell leader had passed her down a bleacher as if she were not a human, but a rolled-up carpet. That was one of the most mortifying experiences of her life. It was exactly the kind of thing she had worked and worried and willed to avoid. Dutch held out his hands. He beat his chest. He wailed to the crowd and came closer.

Desperate, Page threw herself against Doug. "Doug!" she pleaded.

Doug's arms clamped around Page, protectively, as if a bomb might go off. "It's just a joke," he soothed in a worried voice. "It's okay."

"I know. I know."

"AUAUAUAUAOOOO!" Dutch Savage raised his club, and Page grabbed Doug's waist, burying her face against his T-shirt. Doug clutched her even more tightly and then came the strangest thing that had happened during the whole strange night. Page felt herself melt into Doug. Her cheek matched up with the bare skin of his neck, his shaggy hair mingled with hers, even the slight tan on his arms mixed well with her paleness. She wasn't listening to Dutch Savage any longer, and actually she wasn't sure that the wrestler was still there. She was only aware of the wonderful, soothing, fuzzy feeling of being so close to Doug, and the extraordinary knowledge that he felt equally close to her.

"I'm okay," she finally whispered.

"I know you are," Doug replied.

A moment later Page peeked out. Dutch was far away, climbing over the ring ropes, snarling at Magnificent Maurice. She wondered when Dutch had forgotten her. No one was watching her now. Except Doug.

"Thanks," she said, a little shaky.

She expected a wisecrack, but Doug merely smiled. They were suddenly both aware of how they were entwined. Politely, tentatively, Page pulled an arm away. Doug removed a hand. Page inched back to her own seat. Doug cleared his throat and sat up.

"Are you all right?" he asked, over the cheers and boos of the crowd.

"Yes." Page was feeling stranger and stranger. Short of breath. Lazy. A little confused and almost dizzy.

Doug took her hand, then seemed embarrassed that he'd taken it. "I'm sorry I brought you here. I knew it would be pretty lowlife and I guess I did it on purpose. Just to shock you."

"It's okay," Page said, unable to keep the words from tumbling out. "I'm having a great time."

"You are?"

She shrugged, and couldn't stop smiling.

During the final match, Page screamed her heart out for Magnificent Maurice. Dutch pulled some pretty low maneuvers — including jumping the referee — but in the end, Maurice was as magnificent as his name.

After it was all over, she and Doug both moved slowly, hazily, as if they were strolling through cotton candy. On the way home they talked a lot more than they had on the way there, and this time they sat close together. It was amazing. Page realized that it was the first time she had really felt close to a person since her friendship freshman year with Laurel. In fact, by the end, she felt so good that she sang along with Doug and the tape player. When she blew the high notes and Doug pointed at her, no matter how hard Page tried, she couldn't wipe the dopey grin off her face.

It wasn't until they drove up the dirt road leading to her house that she sat up straight and slid back over to her side of the seat. Right away she saw the light on in Whitney's window and old thoughts rushed back into her brain. What Whitney would think. Her will. Laurel. Her class, and making a fool out of herself, and

. . . the strangest thought yet . . . whether or not Doug would kiss her good-night.

Page blushed and reached for the door handle.

Doug gently touched her arm and she froze. They both sat very still, with no sound except their breathing, for what seemed like a long, long time. Finally Page shifted, folding her hands in her lap and staring down at them.

Doug said, "You know, I had a really good time." He sounded a little nervous.

"Me, too."

"Honest?"

Page nodded.

"Wow." Doug tapped her toe with his. "I know this whole thing has been kind of weird for you. I just think it's good not to do what people expect. It turned out okay. Didn't it?"

"I told you I had a good time."

"Oh, yeah. You did, didn't you."

"I did."

"So what do you say we do something tomorrow?"

"Tomorrow?"

"I'm a don't-waste-time kind of guy."

"What kind of a guy aren't you?"

Doug grinned. "Hey, a joke! You'd better watch out. I'm having an effect on you."

Page blushed. Doug was having more than just "an effect" on her. Somehow this whole evening was so disorienting that she felt like a totally different person. She glanced back toward the house. Whitney had just opened the door and was backlit by the bright hall light. Page considered clamping down, running out of the car, doing what Whitney would expect of her. But for some reason, she just couldn't do it. "Tomorrow I have to go on that college trip, with the class. To Berkeley. The college trip."

"I want to go to college. I'll come, too."

Before she knew it she'd said, "Oh, great!" She'd said it an awful lot louder than she meant to. Then something strange happened. It was a combination of that buzzy feeling she'd been having all evening, and those old flashes she'd get just before she got up in front of the whole school. She had a vision of herself lunging across the seat and kissing Doug. A crazy vision of sweeping up Doug in her arms, like a reverse tango or the cover of some corny romance novel. The craziest thing was that she loved this vision. She wasn't afraid of it. After such a nutty evening, nothing seemed too wild or foolish. The vision so amused and delighted her that she began to giggle loudly.

Doug looked around, trying to locate the joke. "Did I do something funny?"

She giggled harder. Then, without thinking, she threw herself across the seat, and kissed Doug so fast and hard that she wasn't sure if she'd even hit his mouth, or possibly broken his teeth.

His blue eyes popped open and this time, he looked stunned. Flabbergasted. Shell-shocked.

"I was just taking your advice," she gasped. "I bet you didn't expect that." Leaving Doug speechless, she jumped out of the car and ran all the way to the house.

CHAPTER 11

"It's too early."

Bets yawned. She heard the window shade snap. When the light hit her eyes, she yanked the blankets back up and burrowed. She had that sleepy, can't-wake-up feeling inside her head that felt like a soft cloud. It was a feeling she'd been getting lately when she had to get up for school. Of course this was still vacation, but the thought of traveling down to Berkeley made her want to stay under the covers all day, watching soap operas and game shows.

"Rise and shine!" Micki encouraged. She was in the bunk above Bets, and swung all the way over so that her face was upside down and her hair almost touched Bets's mattress.

"Go away."

"Bets." Micki popped back up to her own bunk and scrambled around for her watch. When she found it she squealed, "Yikes.

Thompson is going to be here pretty soon. We'd better hurry up."

Bets put the pillow over her head. With her eyes closed, the previous night at the movies replayed in her head. Not the actual film — she couldn't remember much of that. But Greg. She thought about his square jaw and how he smelled like popcorn. It was odd, but she couldn't remember much more about him. She flashed on how he'd gone back with his guy friends, as soon as the movie was over. She wondered when she'd see him again. But she didn't want to think about it for very long, so she pretended that she had fallen back asleep.

Micki wasn't buying it. She sang reveille. "Doo, doo, doo, doo, doo . . ."

"Okay, okay," Bets finally mumbled from under the pillow.

"Bets, it's a beautiful day."

"I don't know why we have to leave so early."

"Ask Thompson." Micki swooped down again and stole Bets's pillow.

When Bets moaned, Micki began bouncing on the bunk and beeping her watch alarm.

Bets thought Micki was going to break the bunk, but luckily Laurel showed up at the bedroom door and calmed things down. Laurel, who'd been sleeping in the tiny back bedroom, was already dressed. Her hair fell in a straight wet line. She was wearing a long skirt with pictures of cellos on it and her soft denim jacket.

"Laurel, why are you ready so early?" Micki asked. She bypassed the bunk bed ladder and simply jumped down to the floor. Then she dangled her watch. "You didn't have an alarm."

"I woke up early anyway." Laurel looked almost as excited as Micki. "Your mom went to see her quilting friend in Crescent Bay," she told Bets. "She dropped me at the bakery and I walked back with some stuff for us."

"Nothing healthy I hope," grinned Micki.

"Just for me." Laurel laughed. "I got some carrot muffins. But I got croissants for you and Bets. And I made some oatmeal."

"Great."

"I'm not hungry," Bets groaned.

Micki and Laurel looked at each other.

"Ready, set . . . GO!"

At the same time, they jumped on Bets, threw off her covers, and dragged her into the kitchen. Bets almost tripped over her flannel nightgown, but once she was finally out of bed the smell of croissants and oatmeal made her feel more alive.

After depositing Bets at the kitchen table, Micki joined Laurel at the counter and started making tea. Since Bets had been acting so low, Micki had been forced to take over some of Bets's old duties — like feeding people. It was funny that even Laurel was filling the void now, too.

"How do I do this, Bets?" Micki asked, holding up the empty teapot. "Do I warm the pot first? I can never remember."

Bets scratched her head, making wisps of hair stand up like yellow sticks. "Um, Micki. You can't warm the pot after you put the tea in."

Micki thought for a minute. As clever as she

was, she could be hopeless at simple things like making breakfast. "Oh, right." She stuck the teapot under the hot water faucet and looked out the window. The fog was lifting and she could see the far-off white-trimmed blue of the rolling water. "What did you think of the movie last night?"

Bets didn't answer and Micki wasn't sure whether to pursue it. Part of her wanted to confront Bets right then and there and have a heart-to-heart. She knew that Bets had made out with Greg at the movies because, well, everybody who went upstairs at the movies supposedly made out. And besides, she'd seen Greg in the parking lot afterward, bumping the other guys with his elbow and whispering. But Bets barely knew Greg! First Kevin, now Greg.

"You should have sat with us, Bets," Micki said.

Laurel brought Bets some oatmeal. Bets dipped her spoon into it, then dropped blobs of oatmeal back into the bowl. "Greg asked me to sit with him."

Micki chewed her croissant and reminded herself to keep her mouth shut. She hadn't ever had a boyfriend, so who was she to talk? Maybe Greg and Bets were destined to be the next major couple at Redwood. Micki didn't know Greg all that well, but he was handsome and a senior. Maybe he was just what Bets needed. "Laurel, what did you think of the movie?"

Laurel smiled and joined them at the table. "I didn't follow the story that well because I kept watching so many other things."

"What other things?"

"Well, I read this article about art directors in one of those catalogues."

"One of my catalogues?"

Laurel nodded. She was talking and eating so intently that crumbs were dribbling down her chin. "In movies, the art director sets up the background, all the props, how everything on the screen looks. So I really got into thinking about that. I want to talk to somebody at Berkeley today to find out more." Laurel laughed, almost choking on her muffin. "Thompson had lots of opinions about the movie, though."

"Thompson has lots of opinions about everything," Micki cracked. "I couldn't believe he thought the plot was dumb. It made him so mad that the guy impresses the snotty rich girl by taking her out on that fancy date and buying her diamond earrings. He said she should have gotten to know the hero guy first, and liked him for who he was." She blew her nut-colored hair out of her face and frowned, thinking over what Thompson had said. "He drives me crazy."

"I thought you didn't care what Thompson thought," Laurel teased.

Micki shrugged and then a smile crept over her face. "Then he started saying how the rich girl wasn't honest with the guy in the movie, and connecting it to this new topic we have for debate. We got into an even bigger argument about that."

"He just talks as much as you do," said Bets.

Laurel and Bets looked at each other and then started giggling. Micki didn't mind a joke at her expense, especially since it had cheered Bets up. "You'll see," she told them, "as soon as we get in the car today, he'll start up again. Mr. Know-it-all."

Micki got up and put the mugs into the sink. In the middle of the suds and the hot water, there was the sound of the screen creaking open and a knock on the front door. "Good morning, Thompson!" Micki yelled. "You can only come in if you keep your mouth shut."

"Or agree with everything Micki says."

They all laughed. "That, too!"

The door opened slowly. Much too slowly for it to really be Thompson. A dark-haired boy stuck his head into the living room, and Laurel shot to her feet.

"Jed!"

"Hello," he said in a quiet voice.

Bets began giggling, clutched at her nightgown, and dashed toward the back bedroom. Micki, who was only in a T-shirt and purple tights, also began backing out of the kitchen. "Hi, Jed. No offense, but we're going to go get showered and stuff."

He nodded and let his dark hair flop over his forehead. "Sure."

After Micki and Bets were gone, the little house echoed with quiet. Laurel was aware of a few birds chirping outside, and her heart beating very quickly, as if she were upset or afraid. Why should she feel anything but joy at a surprise visit by Jed? "Hi. What are you doing here?"

His dark eyes stared down at the sandy carpet.

"I'm glad you're so happy to see me."

"Of course I'm glad to see you." Laurel stepped in closer and put her arms around him. For a moment he just stood there, his hands dangling at his sides. She breathed in the outdoor smell of his long hair, the sunny warmth of his skin. But she also felt his anger. The more intensely she hugged him, and pressed her cheek to his shoulder, the more unresponsive he became. Then finally, when she began to pull away, he grabbed her suddenly and held her so tightly that she could barely breathe.

Laurel finally pulled back, but held onto his hand. "Let's go outside," she urged.

They went out into the front yard. The sun was still rising and gave everything a soft, yellow glow. Laurel and Jed stared at the overgrown plants, the piles of rocks and driftwood, and the grass which had lots of brown patches and weeds. Jed's motorbike was leaning against the outside of the rickety fence. The salty ocean smell was strong.

"What happened with the vineyard job?" Laurel said. "I thought you'd be working today."

"I quit."

"But you just started."

"You know how I feel about working there."

"I know. But Jed, why did you take the job in the first place?"

"Why did you go away for spring break in the first place?"

Laurel was quiet. For a moment she listened to the rhythmic shushing of the waves. Had Jed ridden all the way down here, so early, just to get in a fight? "My dad made me."

"And you're glad he did."

She didn't answer. She *hadn't* wanted to go, and now she was glad she'd come.

Just then, Thompson's mother's Mercedes pulled up into the gravel-and-sand driveway. There was the clacka-clacka noise of the diesel engine idling before it was turned off.

"Helloooo!" Thompson called loudly from the car.

Micki's head popped out of the bathroom window. "C'mon in," she screamed. Her hair was wet and she made a goony face. "But I'm warning you, we're not ready yet."

Thompson jumped out and jogged up to the door. He was wearing a blue pinstriped shirt that had a button-down collar. His khaki pants were creased so perfectly that they looked like the edge of a knife, and they hung perfectly over his polished Bass Weejuns and showed a glimpse of yellow argyle socks.

Thompson noticed Laurel and Jed when he got to the screen door. "Jed, are you coming with us to Berkeley?"

Jed shrugged.

Laurel couldn't help noticing how different Thompson was from Jed. As if Jed was seeing the same thing, he moved further away from the house. Thompson waited for an answer from Jed. When he realized that he wasn't going to get one, he disappeared into the house.

"Why don't you go?" Laurel asked Jed when they were alone again.

"Why? I wanted to spend the day with you. Just ride the bike. Sit on the beach and think of all the things we can do when we get away from this stupid place. If you want to go, you can go without me. I really just came down to give you this." Jed reached in his jean pocket and pulled out a small white box.

It wasn't Laurel's birthday . . . or the anniversary of when they'd gotten together. Jed still wouldn't quite look at her as he handed the box over.

Laurel lifted the tiny lid. It was a ring. A small pink stone on a thin gold band. When she saw the way the stone reflected the sun's sparkle, she could only think that it was perfect, that Jed really loved her, that she was the luckiest girl at Redwood High.

"Jed. It's so beautiful." She wanted to throw her arms around him, but at the same time she just wanted to gaze into his beautiful face.

He was smiling, one of his rare smiles. "Put it on."

She delicately plucked the ring out of the box and slid it onto her finger. But as she and Jed stood staring at it, another thought hit her — Thompson talking about that silly movie last night . . . how giving a present wasn't the same as getting to know someone. Of course that didn't apply to her and Jed. What two people were more on the same wavelength than they were? She knew Jed better than anyone in the world, except maybe her father. And loved him as much.

"It's so beautiful," Laurel gasped. "I can't believe it."

Jed clasped her hand. Hard. So hard that the pressure of the gold band pinched. Laurel was still too swept away to really feel it.

But then another funny thought hit her. A thought that was at once thrilling and something she didn't want to think about for too long. "Jed, does this, I don't know, mean anything?"

He shrugged. "It means whatever we want it to."

Finally he looked at her, really gazed at her face with the full intensity of his dark blue eyes. Laurel felt everything inside her reflecting the warmth and the light just as fully as that cut stone. He pulled her to him, but before they could kiss, Micki, Thompson, and Bets appeared at the front door.

"Time to go!" Thompson announced, leading the way to the car like a camp counselor. Micki jumped in beside him, and Bets climbed more slowly into the backseat. The engine rumbled to life. "Come on, Laurel," Micki ordered from out the window. "Jed, why don't you come, too?"

Laurel stared down at the ring again, although this time she felt herself turning the stone ever so slightly toward her palm. It suddenly occurred to her that this was a real ring, not a dime-store fake. Jed barely had enough money to buy art supplies and gasoline for his bike. He had almost no money saved up for college. Was this why he'd taken that awful job on the vineyard? She looked back at Thompson and Micki, at the Mercedes and the glimpse of Bets slumping in the backseat.

"Let's go," Micki urged.

Laurel tugged on the belt loop of Jed's jeans and whispered, "Jed, what do you think?"

"I came down here to be with you."

Thompson honked the horn. "Come on! We've got to get going!"

"Go on," Laurel finally called, stepping even closer to Jed and clinging to him. His arm clamped over her shoulder in response. "I'm not going."

"Laurel. Why don't you both come?" Micki urged, sounding almost angry. "There's room."

"We don't want to. Go ahead."

The car waited for a minute. Micki rolled down her window and Laurel thought that she was about to open the door and burst out. But at the last second, Micki shook her head and waved good-bye. The Mercedes zoomed away.

CHAPTER 12

Time had never moved so slowly. Driving down to Berkeley Doug felt as if the entire world was still asleep. The freeway traffic seemed to be moving through jelly. Tunes that he heard a thousand times sounded sluggish. Even the palm trees wiggled to the breeze in slow motion.

"Let's go, let's go! Let's get there, be there. Hain is the way to heaven."

Doug snapped his fingers and improvised song lyrics. Lately he'd been trying to write songs with a few buddies from jazz band. Ideas came to him at such weird times that he'd jot them on the inside of his locker or the back of his arm. Today words came so fast that they were gone before he could even remember them. His thoughts were flying, crackling quick as lightning. He could probably have made it from Redwood Hills to Berkeley on mental energy alone.

Maybe even have circled the globe in his Caddy in forty minutes.

"Berzerkley at last. Trolley me up Telegraph," he rapped to himself, as he finally pulled off the freeway and onto University Avenue. "Ten more minutos."

He considered a countdown. Naming the capital of every state. Every student in the Class of '89. A hundred bottles of beer on the wall. Anything! to make these last few minutes move so he could see Page again.

Page.

Doug had always known that he was a little crazy, but now he felt as if he were truly going bonkers. Every girl strolling on the sidewalk reminded him of Page. Not that any of them looked like her. Very few girls were lucky enough to look like Page. And yet, when Doug pictured Page's face, he didn't think of a perfect face on a billboard or a magazine cover. He just thought of Page. Page with the intelligent eyes. Page with that goofy look where her mouth was half open. Page with that wild giggle that sounded like a squawk.

Page had gone to Berkeley that morning on the Class of '89 bus — the bus that she'd organized. The college open house was available to high school students from all over California, so people could also go on their own. They were all meeting in front of the admission hall, which meant Doug driving down alone, and having to wait a minor lifetime before he could see Page again.

Doug managed to take his eyes off the sidewalks and followed the "high school open house" signs instead. The signs led him up Telegraph Avenue, past the stereo stores and fast food places. He also went past bookstores and coffeehouses and storefront campaign headquarters for the upcoming Presidential election. Doug's thoughts were racing so furiously that he'd parked in the special high school lot and was following the arrows to the admissions office without quite realizing it. He was still mumbling song lyrics and running, when he heard someone yell his name.

"YO! MR. MARKANNAN!"

Doug stopped and his insides changed speed as he recognized Thompson's clear voice. Thompson was standing in front of the admissions office lawn with Micki and Bets. In the last few days Doug had almost forgotten about Thompson and Micki and Bets . . . almost.

Micki and Thompson went back to arguing over a campus map, while Bets jogged to meet Doug by herself. Doug's heart sagged a little as he watched her. She wore a faded jumper and baggy sweater, as if she knew she should dress up for this occasion, but hadn't really put her heart in it. There were creases of worry on her freckled forehead, and her usually relaxed, lanky way of moving seemed self-conscious and stiff.

"Yo, Bets."

She halted a few feet away from him, stopping herself from getting too close. Doug lunged toward her and tousled her hair, she slapped his hand away and finally smiled.

"Hi," she whispered. "We didn't know if you'd be here."

"I wouldn't miss it. After all, this is the land of greater learning."

"Oh, boy." Bets didn't hide her lack of enthusiasm.

Doug had the urge to put his arms around her, but he didn't want to give her the wrong impression. When they were younger he'd have given anything for the opportunity of comforting Bets. He used to worry that she never took him seriously, that he was too much of a clown. Now he worried that she would misinterpret his joking, and be misled into thinking he was still in love with her.

"How's, um, stuff back in Redwood Hills?"

A large whoop of joy formed inside Doug as he flashed on his date with Page. But when he looked into Bets's watery brown eyes, he forced his excitement down and answered, "Normal. The same."

Bets twisted her hands in her sweater pockets and nudged the ground with her boot. "Oh. Thompson, uh, he said you had a development, or something like that."

"Did he?" Doug made a muscle-man pose, showing off a scrawny bicep. "I am fully developed," he joked in a deep voice. "Have been for some time."

He was relieved to have made Bets laugh, and to have avoided the real issue. But then he saw Micki and Thompson approach and for the first time his racy excitement hit a standstill. Micki wore an electric-pink sweater. She carried a stack of pamphlets and books and her face beamed with optimism. It occurred to him that Micki and Page were a lot alike. Not that he'd ever had romantic feelings for Micki, and of course Micki was loud and bubbly whereas Page was reserved and cool. But they were both smart and stubborn, determined and tough. Too stubborn to figure out why the feud between them had ever started, and too stubborn to forget about it and let it go. He was beginning to realize how hard it might be to fit these two parts of his life together.

"Where's Laurel, Mick?" Doug asked immediately, hoping to take his mind off Page.

Micki frowned. "She went somewhere with Jed. It's going to be great if her father asks me what we did here."

"Just tell him what you did, and don't even mention Laurel," Thompson volunteered. "It's like what we were talking about last night." Thompson reminded Doug, "Our debate topic for when we get back. I told Micki that each case would have to be decided on its own merits. Sometimes it might be okay to lie for a friend."

"Thompson, the truth is the truth. There's no different truth!" Micki argued.

"What if someone was running for school office and you knew that they had shoplifted once? Once. They knew it was wrong, and would never do it again. Do you tell on them and get them disqualified?"

"That's the same argument you used last night! Thompson, you are so predictable. I hope I get assigned to debate you when we go back to Steinberg's class. I'll know your whole strategy."

Doug let Micki and Thompson hash it out, while Bets gave a sad huff, and finally wandered over to wait on the lawn by herself. Doug was about to point out that the real debate was over why Micki and Thompson made such a big deal out of goading one another. But suddenly he spotted Page and he was glad for the distraction. Page stood on the admission hall steps in a pale blue skirt, white blouse, and ribbon bow tie. Her Class of '89 admirers surrounded her. Doug gasped. His whole physiology clicked into high gear again.

"Doug-o, what tactic are you going to take?" Thompson asked. "Do you think you always have to tell the whole truth, and nothing but, where your friends are concerned?"

"I haven't really been thinking about debate," Doug said. That was true, although it started to seep into his thoughts at that moment. He realized that he hadn't told Thompson the whole truth on the phone. He'd avoided mentioning Page. And even now, he was lying — pretending that he wasn't aware of Page when his whole body felt nothing but her presence.

Just then Micki noticed Page, too. "Look who's here. Gee, maybe we should take the Page Hain tour. We can't possibly figure this place out on our own."

"Are you going off on your own?" Doug said hopefully.

"I'm sure not having anything to do with Page's crowd," Micki laughed. "I can imagine if she saw the four of us. She'd probably arrange to have us blacklisted — but she'd make sure that everyone still thought she was a saint."

"Why would she do that?" Doug asked, trying to sound nonchalant.

"Oh, come on," Micki came back. "Even after all this time, she still loves to get me down." She caught herself. "Never mind — I'm not getting hung up about this. I can handle it. I'm even going to her party. But when she starts in with my friends, that does get to me."

"What are you talking about?"

Micki moved closer to Doug so that Bets wouldn't hear her. "Her party and all the stuff she planned for spring break. It ruined Bets's plans. Bets isn't even having her spaghetti dinner because so many people stayed in town. She was really disappointed. For all I know, Page lured you back to Redwood Hills just to spite us." Micki laughed at the absurdity of her joke, then moved away to banter with Thompson.

Doug knew that Micki was being intentionally ridiculous, but the seed of truth in her statement made him feel as if someone had just buried him in a truckload of mud. He wasn't usually a paranoid person, but he felt a sudden itch of doubt. What if Page was lying? Setting him up to get back at Micki somehow?

He hadn't thought about Micki when he'd asked Page out. Usually, he leapt . . . and then thought about looking when it was way too late. This time he hadn't looked at all. He'd thrown himself off a cliff, and discovered that he could fly. But suddenly, as much as he was soaring, there was a little corner in his brain beginning to warn him that he just might crash.

"Doug, are you coming with us?" Micki had forgotten about Page and instead had that conquer-the-world look. Thompson was concentrating on his map now, neatly marking places of interest with a sharp red pencil. Bets had finally dragged herself up from the lawn and joined them.

Doug didn't answer. He was too busy wondering if this whole thing with Page had been a figment of his bizarre imagination. He hadn't been able to stop thinking about Page kissing him. The memory made him so dizzy he could barely stand, and yet something about the kiss seemed so odd now. The way she had done it — like a commando sneak attack. He wished that he'd kissed her back so that he had more of a sense of how she really felt. Part of him was so totally charmed by the way she'd thrown herself at him, and practically given him a swollen lip, but another part of him worried that Page was really more sophisticated than that and it was all a big joke. Wouldn't that be a laugh? The joker is the butt of the world's biggest yuk.

"Doug-o," urged Thompson. "Let's go. We're not going to learn very much standing here staring at each other." He made a face at Micki. "We can do that in Redwood Hills."

Doug panicked. He wished that he could talk to Thompson alone. Under his sharp, preppy exterior, Thompson was thoughtful and perceptive. But Doug didn't want to make a scene and he didn't want to spend the day with Micki and

Bets. Not until these doubts had been proven, or erased from his head. He had to find out if this thing with Page was true or false. "You guys go ahead without me. I'm going to do my Michael Jackson imitation for the music department and I don't want to embarrass you."

Micki rolled her eyes but was too excited about college to argue with him. "You do that, Doug-o. Come on, Bets. We don't need Page Hain to show us about college. Unless we want to major in refrigeration trucks." She and Thompson led Bets away.

Doug cringed.

Page waited for the Class of '89 crowd to finally break up. She pretended to be busy. She peeked when no one was looking. She prayed. She pleaded that the wonderful thing that had happened between her and Doug wasn't some cruel scheme to make her look like a fool.

"Page," insisted Cindy White, "let's go to the business school first, and then I saw this darling boutique just off campus."

"I want to go to the gym," said Mary Beth Dubrosky.

"We have to stop at the math department," added Mary Beth's twin sister, Alice.

"You go your own ways," Page told them. "I have to stick around and wait for latecomers." She hid her list so that they wouldn't know that she was lying. Everyone who'd signed up had made the bus. There was no one to wait for. Except Doug.

Cindy and the twins continued trying to talk

Page into going with them, but Page merely stuck on her presidential smile and stared out across the admission hall lawn. Doug was still there. His blond hair glistened in the sun and he was wearing one of his goofy T-shirts under a sports jacket that was too big. She'd seen him talking to Micki. Now Micki was gone, and Doug was still waiting.

"We all want to find out about different things," Page insisted, hoping that the girls would leave her alone. "It really makes the most sense to split up."

"Oh, all right," Cindy finally agreed, disappointed.

"Okay," huffed Alice.

"We'll see you later," waved Mary Beth as she accompanied the others down the sidewalk. She called back, "Your speech was great, Page."

"Thanks." Page hugged her clipboard and closed her eyes. She'd made a speech on the bus about what they were supposed to get from this day, and how they had to be determined and ask lots of questions. It was one of her hardest speeches ever. She'd had those crazy thoughts again. Only this time she didn't worry about doing something foolish. This time her crazy thoughts were full of uncertainty and hurt. Her crazy thoughts kept coming back to Whitney.

Last night Whitney had been waiting for her. Page had put all her effort into hiding Doug from her sister when he picked her up. But by the end of that nutty, magical evening, her will wasn't strong enough to keep up the smoke-screen. Whitney had seen the car drive up. She'd recognized Doug. She'd even seen Page kiss him.

"What were you doing out with him?" Whitney had demanded as soon as Page hit the entry hall.

Page had felt too fuzzy and euphoric to answer.

Whitney jumped on her. "Are you insane? After all the work I've done getting people to take you seriously, you waste your time on that clown? He hangs out with Micki Greene! You know she's never forgiven you for taking over as class president. It's probably a setup, just to make you look like a fool."

Whitney's words were still stinging Page's brain, when she opened her eyes and saw Doug walking toward her. She tried to read his blue eyes. His easygoing humor was missing. She looked away. Or maybe he'd looked away first. She thought of leaving, but her feet wouldn't move. A moment later he was standing on the steps next to her. No one else from the Class of '89 was still around.

"Hi."

"Hi."

"I made it." He seemed nervous.

"Yes."

"You made it, too."

"Yes."

"We both made it."

Page nodded.

Suddenly Doug let out a huge sigh. He rumpled his hair with an angry hand and said, "Page,

I don't think I can take having to start this whole thing all over again. If you don't want to hang out with me, just say so. If not, that's okay, too. Just don't be weird. Okay?"

"I want to hang out with you," she gushed, unable to stop herself. "Why do you think I'm waiting here? Besides, you're the weird one."

"I am?"

"Yes. Believe me. I know."

"Well, you didn't have to encourage me by laughing at my jokes. Only weird people laugh at my weird jokes."

She began to smile. "You're the one who wants to major in pro wrestling."

"What do you mean? I think I have a very promising future."

All thoughts of Whitney were being chased out of her head. What was it about Doug that could reassure her so quickly? Whatever, it was exhilarating. And scary. "Well, what are we waiting for? Let's walk around this place. Your brilliant career depends on it. And so does mine."

"I'm waiting for one thing." Doug looked away, almost shy all of a sudden. "Actually, there's one thing I want to do. Need to do."

"What?"

Doug stepped closer and Page felt a force field so strong that she knew there was no breaking this electrical connection. He took one quick glance around, then gently put his hands on Page's shoulders. His eyes closed and he slowly leaned in to kiss her. She felt herself melt into him again. This was no sneak attack. This was a scheduled landing, with everything prepared. This feeling was right on schedule, so right that Page wouldn't have cared if the entire class was standing around laughing at the strangeness of her pairing up with weird Doug.

When they both caught their breath again, Page saw that no one was standing around — except for a few college students. Doug grabbed her hand and they swung arms as they hopped down the steps. "It's going to work," he said, almost to himself.

"Is it?" Page breathed hopefully.

Doug threw back his head and grinned up at the sky. "It has to work. It's that weird."

CHAPTER
13

They giggled. They goofed around. They gawked and pawed at one another like lovesick puppies. It was enough to make Whitney want to throw up.

"Doug, catch!"

"Wait." Doug scrambled across the tasting room. "Page Hain has the crepe paper and she's up on the ladder for the pass. Will she be able to complete it? Markannan is on the move. He's an on-the-move kind of guy. She makes the throw, and it's complete! He runs. He dodges Dutch Savage and Shauna the She-Devil and throws himself over the line!" Doug ran for the crepe paper and carried it, streaming around the room while Page laughed.

Whitney cringed. It was the day after the Berkeley excursion, and they were decorating for Page's party that evening. Whitney still couldn't believe that weird Doug had shown up.

She couldn't believe that Page had welcomed his help — especially after the lecture she'd given her two nights ago. And she was completely disgusted by the stupid lovey-dovey way they were acting. Whitney didn't know how much longer she could watch her little sister throw herself away.

"Will you two pay attention to what you're doing?" Whitney demanded. She was blowing up balloons and her cheeks hurt. "This isn't even my party, and I'm ending up with all the work."

Page had climbed down from the ladder and was twisting her arm away from Doug, while he twisted her in a roll of crepe paper. She wore a pair of beige overalls and an old shirt of their grandfather's. "Whitney, don't help if you don't want to. I never asked you to."

"Great," Whitney grumbled, fuming with frustration. "Don't help. Sure. I'd like to see what this party would look like without me. You barely gave it a thought before this morning."

"Whitney, it doesn't matter how it looks. It's a party, not a decorating show."

Whitney did not agree. How things appeared were very important to her: more and more important as she faced that terrifying unknown of life after high school. If stupid Doug weren't around, she would have sat her sister down and explained that she'd invited friends of her own to the party that night, including two powerful girls from a sorority at Julianne's college. The *only* sorority worth joining. She could just imagine what they would think if they saw these half-baked decorations, and her sister prancing around with a boy who acted like a cross between Billy Crystal and Curious George.

Doug and Page were kneeling in front of the stereo now, both draped with crepe paper. He'd brought over a stack of his jazz records and he put on what sounded like a big band. It reminded Whitney of something her parents would dance to.

"You're not going to play that tonight, are you?"

Doug had this playful look in his eyes that seemed to mock her. It drove her crazy. "It's up to Page," Doug said. "Pebbles, what do you think? It's your party. I brought lots of records."

Page pulled him up and they began an impromptu jitterbug. "I think . . . we can play all kinds of music."

Whitney hated big band music. She hated Doug. And she hated seeing her sister act like such a fool. It was Saturday, the end of spring break. On Monday they'd be back at Redwood, and for Whitney that meant the downslide to the end of senior year. Next year she was entering the great unknown and she felt as if her entire life were slipping out of her grasp.

But she knew how to get it back. Plan. Arrange. Scheme. Maybe some girls thought scheming was a bad thing, but Whitney knew that they just weren't smart enough to be successful at it. Whitney had meticulously planned her high school career from the moment it started. When she was a freshman she'd picked the second prettiest girl in the Class of '88 to try out with her for a sure cheerleading victory. Celia Cavenaugh. Whitney had eventually dumped Celia. But what mattered was that she had planned that cheerleading tryout down to the color of her shoelaces. And she'd won. She'd even made ungrateful Celia win, too.

Whitney gave one last, agonizing puff into a balloon, then let it go and watched it fly around the room. She couldn't hear the whine, because Doug had put another record — some woman named Billie Holiday, whose singing was so laid back she sounded barely alive. Page didn't see the balloon flying around because she was so busy goofing around with Doug.

"Where's Jed?" Whitney almost shouted, pushing aside the balloons and tape and string. "I thought Roy hired him to help us set up."

Page turned down the stereo and looked over at her. "Jed quit the same day he started work. Dad told me. I guess he didn't like it."

"That figures." Whitney shook her head. Jed was a good lesson in what could happen when you didn't plan and scheme. Then you were open to all kinds of forces. Infatuation with the worst possible boy. At least Page was no longer buddies with that dreary Laurel. Whitney had seen to that last year. "He's such a nothing."

"Whitney, think about it," Doug challenged. "Don't you honestly think it might be better for Jed not to work here? It must be weird enough for him to live out on the vineyard."

Whitney gritted her teeth. She was not going to get into a battle with Doug. He wasn't even worth her anger.

As if he were on the same wavelength, Doug slung an arm around Page and said, "How about taking a break and getting something to eat at the D.Q.?"

Page, who had a secret passion for junk food, immediately dragged him to the door. "Okay. Whitney, we'll be right back. You don't have to do this if you don't want to."

"Who, me? I don't mind."

"You want anything?"

Whitney resisted the impulse to scream. "No. Thank you."

Doug and Page waved and giggled and finally left.

Fine, Whitney told herself. Let Doug and Page traipse down to the stupid Dairy Queen to eat stupid soft ice cream that you might as well plaster right on your thighs. She would stay here and sip Diet Pepsi. She would twist and arrange the crepe paper until it looked like the senior prom. She would keep her eyes open at the party tonight, and plan the rest of Page's junior year before it was too late. Before the Hain sisters looked like total fools.

On the other side of Redwood Hills, a wood-paneled Jeep Wagoneer was pulling into the busy streets of downtown. The Wagoneer was as cluttered as the neighborhood. It contained three high school girls, one mom, and a spring break's worth of sandy towels, damp bathing suits, jars of leftover jam and hot dog relish.

Laurel sat in the backseat with Micki. As usual, her eyes were busy. There was a lot to look at. The downtown streets flickering by. Micki next to her in the backseat, scribbling in her hot-pink notebook. Bets shifting moodily in the front seat, and Bets's mother nodding her head to a country tune on the radio.

But Laurel saw most of her surroundings as a blur, as if they were the background for one of her drawings, and she had smudged them with the side of her fist. The only thing her eyes really fastened on was the ring from Jed. She wore it on the same hand as the woven bracelet they had bought together last summer. The ring was twisted inward, hiding the sparkle from the other girls, and from herself.

"Do I turn here?" Mrs. Frank asked.

"Yes. Please."

Bets and Micki perked up as Laurel's modern white apartment complex came into view. The walls were low and made of something that glittered under the noon sun. Laurel felt the stone on the inside of that ring again and looked out to see if her father was waiting in front. Luckily he wasn't.

Luckily the other girls hadn't noticed the ring, either. By the time she got back from her day with Jed, Micki and Bets were ready to crash. Micki was pooped from reading every word in every catalogue, and Bets was worn out from watching the clock and waiting for Greg, who had never shown up. Laurel was relieved not to have to explain the ring to them. She wasn't sure what it meant herself. The woven bracelets she and Jed wore had been bought for three dollars each, and they didn't really mean anything . . . except that they belonged together. They matched. They shared something that no one else could share. But this was another story. A real ring that Jed couldn't afford. A ring that grown-up people gave for engagements and weddings. Just thinking about it made Laurel want to retreat to her old hiding places.

"This is it," she pointed out to Bets's mom.

By the time the girls finished their good-byes, Laurel's dad had appeared. He rushed down the steps and opened the car door, pulling out Laurel's duffel bag and swinging it over his shoulder. He looked the same as ever in his Mexican sweater and sandals and patched blue jeans. But when Laurel got out and hugged him, he only half hugged her back.

"Did you have a good time?" he leaned into the car to ask Micki and Bets. He avoided looking at Laurel. "How was Berkeley?"

Bets rubbed her eyes and Micki stared down at her notebook. Laurel was grateful to Micki for not saying anything. And yet, her father knew these girls. She wondered if he realized that tight lips from Michelle Greene were like a rampant lie from anyone else.

Laurel filled in the pause herself. " 'Bye. Thanks, Bets. Thanks, Mrs. Frank." She wanted to say thanks to Micki, too, but she didn't dare. Instead she touched Micki's arm through the window and hoped that Micki understood.

Everyone waved as the Wagoneer pulled away. Laurel waited until it was gone, then turned back to her father. But he and her duffel bag were gone. Laurel saw a glimpse of his back as he rounded the corner toward their apartment. Everything about him, from the way he'd hugged her to his quick, stiff exit spelled out that something was wrong. Laurel slowly followed, feeling a kind of dread and awkwardness she hadn't felt since the last time she'd had to stay with her mother and her stepfather.

Her dad had left the front door open. Her duffel had been dropped under the breakfast bar and he was flicking off the New Age music he always listened to. His books and records were scattered in front of the fruit crates they used for shelves, and he stepped over them to sit on the sofa.

"We have to talk," her father said right away.

"Sure." Laurel sat on the carpet opposite him. Nervously, she folded her slender hands on the tree-trunk coffee table. "Is something wrong?"

He looked as if he'd been up all night worrying. "You didn't go to Berkeley, did you?"

Laurel's breath stopped. She hadn't expected this kind of direct accusation from her father. Her mother, yes. But usually her father was softer and more sympathetic. "Why do you say that?"

He hadn't shaved and light reflected off the specks of gray in his Saturday stubble. "I called Jed yesterday and his uncle told me he went down to the beach. I had the feeling that Jed didn't go to be by himself."

"What were you doing, spying on me?" Her mind was whirring, trying to come up with an excuse, a distraction, anything to avoid the real issue.

"I only called him because somebody at the office was throwing away some old parts. I thought Jed might want them for his sculptures."

"Well, how do you know that Jed didn't go to Berkeley, too?"

"Did he?" her dad asked hopefully.

Laurel let her hair cover her face. She knew that she was in too deep to pull this off.

"That's what I thought," her father answered for her. "I know Jed. He thinks he'll find some magic world out there that doesn't exist. He's not ready to go looking into the real thing." He sighed. "Laurel, you lied to me."

Laurel's throat clutched with tears. "I don't know what to say."

"Don't say anything. Just listen for a minute." He sorted through his work papers on the coffee table and pulled out a large envelope. "I talked to your mother this morning. I told her what was going on with you, and we both agreed that it would be good for you to spend this coming summer away from Redwood Hills."

"The whole summer?"

"The whole summer." He pulled a colorful brochure out of the envelope and pushed it across the tree-trunk table. "There's a program called American Heritage for high school juniors. They have an art study in Italy — in Florence. I signed you up."

"What!"

"Laurel, I know it will be hard for you to go

somewhere on your own. I know it was hard for you to move here and start high school in a new place after the divorce. But, honey, you are so talented and bright. You're only seventeen. You have to make your world bigger. You can't start holding yourself back now."

Laurel stared at the tree-trunk table, her eyes filling with tears. She'd started high school alone. At first she'd had Page as her only friend, but that hadn't lasted. Now Jed was her life. But she also sensed that she could exist in the outside world, too. Maybe some kind of change had occurred over spring break. She'd spent time with Micki and Bets, and Thompson and the others and she hadn't felt lonely. She'd even resented Jed a little bit for showing up yesterday and taking her away. But she wasn't ready for this kind of a break. "I won't go!"

"Laurel, you don't have a choice."

Laurel stared at the brochure. On the cover was a picture of Michelangelo's David, imposed on top of arched bridges and a building that looked like a stone castle. Part of her wanted to see more of that world. But instead, she shoved the pamphlet back. "No!"

"I know you're upset. But once you get used to the idea, I think you'll feel differently."

She felt the ring that she was hiding on her finger, then she stared at the picture on the brochure. Both Jed and her father were going to such extremes. There had to be someplace in between, Laurel prayed. There had to be.

CHAPTER 14

"Do I look okay?" Bets asked.

"You look great."

"Gee, Micki. Really?"

"Bets, I wouldn't lie to you."

"I feel okay. At least, um, sort of great, anyway."

"Good. I don't think anyone should go to a party unless they at least feel sort of great."

Micki and Bets took each others' arms. They were on their way to Page's party, walking from Bets's ranch, which was about a mile away by back unpaved roads. Bets carried a flashlight that waved a beam in front of them. Above was clear, starry sky. All around was the smell of dirt and grapevines and cows. And under their feet the gravel skidded and scrunched.

"We are going to have a good time tonight, right?" bolstered Micki.

"Right."

They began to walk in step. "Follow the yellow brick road."

A cow mooed and Bets mooed back. "Lions and tigers and cows."

"Oh my!"

Bets ran ahead, taking a one-step jump onto a fence post, then leaping gracefully back down. Micki applauded her. She'd seen Bets walk the length of an entire pasture on top of an inch-wide wooden fence — something Micki would never attempt in a million years. She was glad to see a hint of Bets's old athleticism and physical confidence. Maybe Bets was pulling out of her doldrums. Maybe she was forgetting about Greg. Maybe this party was just the thing to usher them into the final months of junior year.

They'd been pepping each other up since they'd gotten back from the beach. Actually, Micki hadn't needed much pepping. In spite of her worries about Laurel and Bets, she was proud of herself. Proud of keeping her mouth shut, of not interfering, or taking sides, or getting involved in things that weren't her responsibility. She had changed since sophomore year, when she used to carry her entire class on her shoulders. She'd really changed.

"There it is." Micki stopped and pointed to the Hain tasting room. It was an imitation Swiss chalet, so lit up and over-decorated that it could have been the wizard's castle in Oz. "Race you over there."

Bets took off. They swerved around Cindy White's Mustang and Paul O'Conner's pickup. Past Doug's Caddy, too; Thompson's mom's

Mercedes, and a red BMW that belonged to some snotty senior who was a friend of Whitney's. Music poured out of the front door. Bouncy brass and voices that were swinging. For a moment Micki thought that Doug and his buddies might have been playing, but even Doug didn't play that well. Of course, Bets made it to the door first. But she waited for Micki to catch up before going in.

"Ready?"

"Okay."

As soon as they walked in, they were greeted by scads of juniors. The loudest were Carlos Oneda, Josh Morgan, and Sarah Parker.

"Look who's here!"

"Micki! Mondo tan."

"How was the beach?"

"Hi, Bets."

The whole crazy Class of '89 was here. Not just the Page followers, but even Micki's friends, and the kids who didn't distinguish between them. Micki even recognized some seniors. As junior year moved forward, the distinctions between crowds were getting looser — in spite of Micki's lists and comparisons. Maybe everybody was mellowing out as much as Micki was, and this party was going to be equally relaxed.

"Micki, I'm going, um, outside," Bets hollered over the music. "To, you know, see who's here."

Micki knew that Bets was going to look for Greg, but she decided to be mellow about that, too. She couldn't help a little giggle to herself when she noticed the decorations. As expected, Page had gone all-out. One part of the floor had even been covered with leaves, and on top of them stood big copper tubs holding masses of spring flowers. Micki thought she'd never seen such a riot of color. In the middle of all that stood a giant papier-mâché grape cluster with the Hain family crest underneath it. It looked so silly that Micki immediately wanted to laugh. Boy, Doug-o was going to have a field day with that one, Micki thought. Doug loved anything oversized and corny — like his parents' Cadillac — when he saw those grapes, Micki knew he'd go bananas.

Where was Doug, anyway? While the other kids were chattering over their spring break adventures, Micki looked around. The stereo was up on a platform twisted in crepe paper and more flowers. The song ended and a sultry trumpet introduced the next cut. Everyone on the dance floor recoupled and rearranged themselves for the slow number.

"Oh, my God."

That was when Micki saw them. She stopped dead and stared, as if all the other dancers were in soft focus and only Doug and Page were clear. Micki blinked. She closed her eyes again and shook her head. She opened them slowly in an effort to make certain that she wasn't hallucinating.

But the vision wouldn't go away. It *was* Doug and Page. They were out in the middle of the floor slow-dancing together. Doug was holding Page close and had a huge smile on his face. He was whispering in her ear occasionally, too. Page, for her part, had an even bigger smile on her face. More than that, she was wearing a careless white dress under a sloppy sweatshirt. The whole picture was so incredibly un-Pagelike that Micki put her hands up to her mouth and gasped. When . . . how . . . why had this happened?

"I don't believe it," she said out loud.

Sarah Parker, who was standing nearby with Josh, caught Micki's remark. "What don't you believe, Mick?"

Micki pointed with one finger at the slow-dancing couple.

"Oh, yeah," Sarah said, running a hand through her purple-streaked hair. "Everybody has been talking about it. They're like glue this evening. Funky couple. Is Doug going out with her?"

"Is he?" Micki was too stunned to be anything more than an echo. She felt as if she had been conked over the head and was just now waking up and the world was totally different. She was disoriented, dizzy, and sick to her stomach. Part of Micki assumed that it had to be a joke, or a dare, or some weird attempt at improving class relations. But then she saw Doug close his eyes and kiss Page's cheek, while Page smiled and nestled even closer to him. Page looked dreamy and not quite in control. Page never looked like that! Not since freshman year, anyway.

"Poor Doug," Micki moaned.

"He doesn't look so bad off to me," Josh answered in a yuk-yuk voice.

"No, you don't get it," Micki replied, not really expecting Josh to get it, since he was known around Redwood for having zero social skills and spending his time in the science lab grafting different branches onto small trees. Page has never forgiven me, Micki wanted to say. Not since I made the horrible mistake of writing awful things in her locker freshman year. She wasn't content to hurt Bets. And she knows that I'm too tough for her. So she's sunk her teeth into Doug.

Just then there was a familiar pointy tap on Micki's shoulder. She knew instantly who it was. When she turned around to look, she saw Thompson wearing a seersucker sportscoat and suspenders over a white shirt and slacks. Micki wasn't sure if he looked like a dashing young man from the nineteen-twenties, or someone who sold ice cream. "What gives with Doug-o and Page-the-pain Hain," she demanded as soon as Sarah and Josh left to join the dancers.

Thompson didn't grin. He merely shrugged and stuck his hands in his pockets. "I just found out about it. I guess it's serious. They were to-gether at Berkeley yesterday. They avoided us genius types. Didn't want to have compete with intellects like ours, I suppose."

"Thompson!" Micki knew she was entering that one-track, emotional place of hers. But still, this was urgent. Thompson should have called her as soon as he found out about it. It was so predictable of him to keep it to himself.

"Mick, it's none of our business."

"This is one thing you don't know anything

about. I can't believe he's serious."

"Believe it, Mick."

Micki was aware of the music again. Slow, sexy jazz. Billie Holiday! Doug was the only person she knew who owned those kinds of records and he almost never loaned those records to anyone! Micki realized that this *was* serious.

"Micki," Thompson said in a sober voice. "Forget about it." His Tom Sawyer grin popped back. "Come on. Let's dance." He tapped his toes. "A slow dance. My chance to cripple you for life."

"How inviting. Thompson, just once, just this once, give me a break. Okay?"

He tried to pull her out onto the floor. Now the look on his face was incisive and very serious. "I am, Micki. You may not know it, but I am. I give you a break whenever I can."

Micki felt like her emotions were on overload. The last thing she needed was know-it-all Thompson complicating things. The weird part was that she had this funny sense that if she did talk this over with Thompson, he would help her to figure a lot of things out.

But she didn't trust him. How could she trust him after she'd started getting those bubbly, frothy feelings when she was around him? That was the part of this thing with Thompson that wasn't predictable, and Micki didn't like it. She'd seen what messes romance got people into. Look at Laurel and Jed. Look at Bets. Look at Doug and Page! Look what a mess she'd made of things by falling hard for a boy freshman year.

"Thompson," she said, breaking away from the dance floor. "Sorry, but I don't feel like dancing right now."

He watched her with that patient, amused look of his. "Suit yourself. You know where to find me when you change your mind."

In back of the tasting room was an arbor, covered with grapevines that scraped in the breeze. Bets was leaning on the outside of it. She was breathing in the cool fresh air, hidden from the boys who sat inside, separated from her by budding vines and a crisscrossed wooden trellis. There were about six guys in there, including Greg, Sam Pond, Paul O'Conner . . . and Kevin. Bets was trying to figure out how to attract Greg's attention, without being seen by Kevin. She felt dumb standing there. Stuck. She had never been very bold to begin with, and seeing Kevin again had frozen her to stone.

"I know it was his best one yet," Sam was bragging.

"Nah. The last one was much better."

"Oh, come on, Kevin. Think about the whole thing. The music. The story. The way it moved. It made the last one look completely lame."

Bets wasn't really listening at first. They were talking about rock videos or episodes of *Miami Vice*, or one of those guy subjects they liked to argue about. Bets turned until her cheek was against the trellis. The wood muffled the music and laughter from inside the house, but she could hear the boys quite clearly. They had that boasty, macho sound to their voices, as if they were trying to outbluster one another.

"I didn't think it was such a great movie, either," said Greg. "Not nearly as good as *Ferris Bueller*."

"Listen to him," howled Sam.

"What?"

"How would you know how the movie was, Kendall?" Sam taunted. "You didn't see any of it."

Now Greg was laughing, too. "Yeah. Well..."

"Wait a minute," objected a voice that Bets didn't recognize. She shifted and saw that it was another senior, Roger Sandler. He was some big deal in the Class of '88. "I thought you all went to see *Some Kind of Wonderful* when you were down at the beach."

Bets froze, almost afraid to breathe. She listened carefully, trying to identify the laughter that was spreading and getting more raucous.

"We did. But Kendall was too busy to watch."

"What can I say?" boasted Greg. "It was one of those nights when ... you just don't feel like watching the movie."

"Hey, hey, hey," sang Roger. "Details. I want details."

The boys moved closer together, as if they were gathered around a poker game.

"She's a junior. Betsy Frank. Pretty cute. I didn't even know her. Just took her upstairs and she was putty in my hands."

"All right."

They all slapped palms and guffawed.

"Get her phone number."

"Ask Michaelson," Greg howled. "He turned me on to her."

Kevin stood up and took a bow. "I admit that I have a superior sense for this kind of thing. You guys all know that." Wolf whistles. Groans. "I was going to give her another go, see just how much she really puts out, but then I met this incredible looker on the beach. Margie. She's a freshman at College of Marin."

The boys went on to rate Margie from Marin, and their voices smacked the inside of Bets's head hard as a handball pounding on an indoor court. She couldn't look at them. She couldn't see. She could hardly breathe, or think, or make a sound. This wasn't her old bricked-up feeling. No, this was as if all that heaviness inside her was exploding. Breaking her heart. Shredding her pride into tiny, splintery sticks.

She clutched her stomach, holding in the hurt and the humiliation. The only thing worse than overhearing what these boys thought of her would be getting caught and having to look them in the face. So she tried to pretend that she was somewhere else. Somewhere safe. Out in the backfield with a new colt. On the freshman year hayride with Doug. Digging in the garden with her mother. She held everything in and prayed that she would be able to escape soon. Because she knew that when she let go, they'd hear her sobs all the way from Redwood High to that movie theater in Ocean City.

Micki was talking about the SAT exams with Nancy Carlin and John Pryble, when she saw

Bets run by outside the tasting room window. She wasn't even sure how she knew that it was Bets, or that something was terribly wrong, except that she was so tuned in to her friends right now. As hard as she tried not to worry, every person at the party made her think of Bets or Laurel or Doug.

"Can you guys excuse me? I'm going to go out and get some air," she told Nancy and John. "Let's talk about this some more when we get back to school."

John and Nancy kept right on comparing horror stories, while Micki made her way through the crowd. She shouldered her way out the door and into the cool evening. For a moment she stood in front of the tasting room, looking out over the parking lot and the fences and the rows and rows of grapes that made soft rustling sounds. Finally she picked out Bets's blonde hair gleaming under a lighted billboard. On the advertising sign was a picture of Page's father, sniffing a glass of wine, looking confident and robust — the opposite of the freckle-faced girl, who was crumpled on a patch of grass, clutching her knees and rocking slightly.

A flash of panic zapped through Micki. She knew right away that something awful had happened. She raced across the lot. Bets was on the other side of the parking lot in a little play area, which was probably there to entertain kids while their parents sipped wine inside. Her back was against the metal post of a swing set, and the empty swing next to her wobbled gently in the breeze.

"Bets!" Micki dropped down next to her. When Bets turned to face her, Micki saw the streams of tears. Bets was quiet until Micki threw her arms around her, and then Bets let go with a wail that surged and shook. Micki wasn't sure what to think at first. She had to assume that it was Doug's stupid infatuation with Page. Why, why had she let things go this far?

"Why didn't you tell me?" Bets sobbed.

"I didn't know," Micki told her. It ripped her heart open to see Bets gasping for breath, her voice coming out in heaves, the tears gushing down her face.

"Greg. And oh, Kevin. And oh, me. Oh, I can never show my face again. I'm so stupid. I hate myself. Why didn't I see it? Why didn't you tell me? I thought you were my best friend?"

Micki was beginning to realize that Bets was distraught over more than Doug and Page. "I am your best friend, Bets. I would do anything for you. You know that. Please, tell me what happened."

"I heard them. They think it's funny. They think I'll go with any boy. They were, oh, laughing, laughing at me."

"Kevin and Greg?"

"Yes! Oh, Micki. I just wanted them to like me. To think I was important, too. I'll . . . I'll never be able to ever show my face at school again. They . . . they all talked about me. They laughed." Her whole body was trembling and heaving.

Micki held Bets as hard as she could. She tried

to wrestle Bets's hurt away with the power of her arms, but the more tightly she held her, the more Bets cried and shuddered and shook.

"It's okay, Bets. I'm here. It's okay."

"Oh, Micki. Why didn't you tell me?"

Good question, Micki accused herself. What kind of a friend was she? She'd seen this coming. She'd known from the start that Kevin was using Bets, and that Greg was just following in his footsteps. She knew that boys could be even more vicious gossips than girls. She was smart enough to know that Bets was scared of college and the future and looking for something else to make her feel she was a success.

Why hadn't she said anything? Had she stood back so far that she wasn't even a good friend anymore?

She held Bets until the tears softened and the sobs turned to shaky breaths and sighs.

"Bets, what do you want me to do?"

"I want to go home."

"Okay. Wait here. I'll be right back. I don't want you walking. I'll get Doug to drive you."

Bets shivered and nodded.

Micki gave Bets one last hug. Once she was back in the parking lot, she could see the dance floor through the window. Luckily Bets was too far away and bleary-eyed to see Doug wrapping himself around Page like streamers round a maypole. And Page throwing her head back and singing along with the music, as if she were really having a good time. Oh, sure. Page hadn't acted like that since Micki had made her dress up as Pebbles Flintstone. Page had clawed her way to power in the junior class, planned everything from spring break activities to her conservative dress-for-success blazers and little bow ties. And she had suddenly decided to make a total turn-around and fall for Doug? Yeah. Right. Micki didn't believe one bit of it.

Micki had stood back for over a year now. She'd let Page take over her presidency. She'd let Laurel deceive her father and throw away her future for Jed. She'd let Bets get taken advantage of and humiliated. Enough was enough. It was time to tell the truth. To start taking some responsibility for her friends again.

"Do what you have to do," she told herself.

Keeping her eye fixed on Doug, Micki stormed her way back into the party. Her quick mouth was ready, and she couldn't wait for Doug to hear what she had to say.

CHAPTER 15

What a mess.

Doug sat in the front seat on the driver's side of his Cadillac. The steering wheel was huge — almost the size of a Hula Hoop. The leather was lush and slick. The rearview mirror was as long as an ice cube tray and the chrome from the radio dial sparkled under the parking lot nights. But for all the incandescent glamour of the Caddy interior, there was no hiding the sadness that was all around him.

"Bets, believe me, they're morons."

"It's all my fault."

"No, Bets."

Bets cried harder. Doug kept handing her more tissues. Fortunately, his mother kept a box of them in the glove compartment. Doug hadn't been counting, but he'd guess that they'd gone through about fifty tissues so far. Nevertheless, Bets kept crying . . . and crying and crying.

Doug felt helpless. Those idiots — Kevin Michaelson and Greg Kendall. Sure, Doug had seen it coming, but it still made him furious. He wasn't the violent macho type, but if he were, he'd have cleaned up on those jerks like an old-time western.

However, Bets was only one part of Doug's dilemma. The other part was Micki. And what she had just told him made him want to join Bets and break into tears himself.

Micki was wrong. There were no two ways about it — WRONG. Still, her warning rang in Doug's ears. Micki had grabbed him at the serving table, where Doug had been waiting for Page to answer Cindy White's questions about the junior prom. From there Micki had pulled him out into the parking lot. At first she had insisted it was about Bets, but then Micki started telling him how Page was making a fool out of him and setting him up for a fall. How could an iceberg like Page really be interested in a joker like him?

Micki was voicing Doug's worst fears, but he refused to believe it. He knew that Micki and Page had been enemies since freshman year, but they were juniors now. It was time to move into the future. What's more, Doug knew that Page was ready to move on . . . at least he assumed she was. They hadn't actually talked about Micki because their relationship had sort of gone from weirdness . . . to jokes . . . straight to romance. Still, he was convinced that Page had put the whole feud behind her . . . hadn't she?

Micki sure wasn't convinced. Doug was being

"naive," he was being "used." He was going to end up hurt just like Bets was hurt, and now Micki was blaming herself that her friends were so dense. It made Doug feel like screaming. Let me be dense! Bets made her own mistakes, and so will I. We'll pay for them. Maybe even learn from them. They're our lives. But then Micki had pointed out Bets at the other end of the parking lot. She was standing in the shadow of one of the big overhead parking lot lights, crying her head off.

Doug's heart had melted. He'd left Micki and immediately had gone over to where Bets was shaking and shuddering. He led her over to the Cadillac and made her get into the front seat. So now they were both sitting there recovering. Bets was trying to get herself together, and Doug was mulling over what Micki had said. Between them were the sniffles, the Kleenex, and the big armrest that folded down in the front seat.

"Bets, are you feeling any better?"

Bets looked over, blew her nose once, and opened her puffy eyes. "A little. Thanks."

"Do you still want me to drive you home?"

"You don't, um, have to."

"It's too late to walk. And I'm sure you don't want to go back to the party."

Bets violently shook her head. "Uh-uh."

"Well," Doug said, "then I think I should take you home." He started to get out. "I'll be back in a sec."

Bets stopped him. "You don't, um, have to

get Micki. I think she wants to stay. You know, to prove to Page that it's not a big deal for her to be here."

Doug scratched his head. That was typical Micki logic when it came to Page — staying at her party to prove that she didn't really care. Doug settled back behind the steering wheel. The thought of going in and confronting Micki again didn't appeal to him. But then he remembered that he wasn't going in to talk to Micki, but to tell Page his plans. He couldn't suddenly ditch Page's party without letting her know what was going on. Maybe he was a joker, but he wasn't an inconsiderate goon.

He was about to explain the whole thing to Bets, when he realized that Bets probably didn't know about him and Page. Between the tears and darkness and the lonely inside of the Cadillac, he felt too close to Bets to pretend or hand her a lie. "Bets, I've got to go tell Page where I'm going," he said in a strong voice. "It won't take very long."

Bets took in a deep breath and it shuddered through her. "Page?" She sniffled. "Oh, you mean to say thanks and all. I guess you should say good-bye for me, too."

Doug smiled sadly. He didn't want to hurt Bets any more on this awful evening, but he also didn't want to drive her home if she thought it meant a resumption of his old, long-gone crush. He made his point again. "Page was my date tonight."

Bets looked up, puzzled. Her eyes were red

as a terrible sunburn, and she kept rubbing them with the backs of her fists. "Page? You and Page?"

"I know it's weird. And it's only been going on for a few days. I don't know."

Her tears didn't well up again. Actually Bets looked a little relieved. She seemed to understand exactly why he'd told her. "It's okay. I'm glad you and I are just friends now. I wasn't before. But now I am. Um, a boyfriend is the last thing I need. For, well, right now, a friend is much better."

Doug put his arm around her and squeezed hard. Finally he had the freedom to show the deep affection he felt for her. As soon as he hugged her, she swung her arms around his neck and began to sob again. Full, free, throaty sobs. It sounded as if Bets was getting rid of all her hurt, so that she could finally be free of it.

"That's it, Bets. I'll sit with you until you go through that whole box of Kleenex, then I'll let Page know what's going on and I'll take you home."

"Okay."

Doug hugged her harder and let her finish her cry.

Page was back in the kitchen, refilling chip bowls and stuffing trash into giant garbage bags.

"Guess what I just heard, Page?" Whitney enticed in her gooiest voice.

Page flinched. She'd been wondering why Whitney was helping with the dirty work. Now she knew. She could tell from the twisted look of her sister's bow mouth that Whitney had some nasty gossip she was dying to unload.

"What?" Page sighed, trying not to listen. Instead she collected empty Pepsi cans and kept her eye out for Doug. In the middle of that stupid conversation with Cindy White, Doug had vanished. Page was sure he'd turn up soon, but she was starting to be concerned.

"Don't pretend you're not interested."

"Actually, I'm not."

Whitney stopped working and leaned back against the counter. "Sorry. I just thought you might be wondering where your friend Doug disappeared to."

Page felt the hairs on the back of her neck tingle. But she kept picking up and neatening. This party was going too well to let Whitney spoil things. Besides, she could think of a dozen logical places for Doug to be right now. Just because this amazing feeling had suddenly erupted between them was no reason why they had to spend every second of her party together. "Not really," she said in the coolest possible voice.

"Oh? I suppose you think he's just perfect for you."

Page stopped. There was a familiar look on Whitney's face, one that Page had seen a million times before. It was a look that said Whitney held the trump card. It was smart; it was powerful; and it was smug. "He's — "

Whitney cut her off. "Before you tell me how

great your new boyfriend is, why don't you go over and ask the guys where Doug is. And what's he doing out there."

"Why?"

Whitney had a barely perceptible smile on her face. "Now you want to know, don't you?"

Page couldn't help herself. "What?"

"Doug — your dear friend, Doug — has been out in his car with Betsy Frank — who, if I am to believe Kevin Michaelson, is the make-out queen of Redwood High."

Page's mind short-circuited. She could barely digest what Whitney was telling her. She felt sick and dizzy and sure that what Whitney was saying couldn't possibly be true. "Bets and Doug are old friends, and she's not a make-out queen. Don't be so horrible."

Whitney pulled Page into a private corner next to the refrigerator. She held on to Page's arm so tightly Page thought she would puncture her with her fingernails. "That's not what Kevin and Greg say about Bets, and believe me, they've had direct experience. I overheard them laughing about it, so I asked and found out everything. Page, I'm only looking out for you. Doug has been in that car with her a long time. I went out and looked myself and they were in each other's arms." Whitney took a step back and held up her right hand. Her gray eyes were as hard as the chrome on the tasting room freezer. "I swear I'm telling you the truth. I swear."

Page shook her head as if she could fling this information away with the sweep of her long hair. She didn't want to believe it. She'd known Bets for three years and even though they weren't close friends, she always had the impression of a sweet farm girl who was content to hide in Micki's shadow. But Cindy White had just been gossiping about the same thing. What had started as a chat about the junior prom had quickly disintegrated into mud-slinging against Bets. Cindy had gotten the scoop from Greg Kendall.

"I tried to warn you before," Whitney reminded, softening with sisterly sympathy. "I think he set you up, Page. He wanted to make you look like a fool. I hate to be the one to say I told you so."

"Leave me alone."

Page left the kitchen. Blindly, bumping elbows with several people and not bothering to apologize. She wasn't sure where she was headed. To the parking lot to see for herself? To find Kevin? Cindy? Micki Greene? NO. She didn't want to see any of those people.

She was next to the dance floor when she saw Doug making his way through the crowd. He was looking around — looking for her, she sensed. He had his jacket bunched up under his arm as if he were on his way out. Part of Page wanted to go to him, but part of her was too scared. What if what Whitney had said was true? What about all the people here that she didn't know — the ones from college, the ones from the sorority. The old Page that cared most of all about what other people thought didn't want her to see Doug anymore. It wanted her to run and never trust any boy, let alone someone as different as Doug.

Suddenly Doug spotted her. Page tried to make her way back to the kitchen, someplace where he couldn't get to her. But there were too many people. As she passed a group of seniors, Greg Kendall reached out an arm and tried to pull her down on his lap. She jerked her arm away and kept on going. Suddenly all she could remember was Doug kissing her when they were at Berkeley. Who knows who could have seen them? Maybe her reputation was as pathetic as Bets's.

"Page!" Doug yelled over the music.

Page turned back and stared right into Doug's face. His blue eyes still moved her, and there was a whole other part of her inside that wanted to say, Forget everyone else. Forget Bets and Micki and Whitney and all my worries about what people think of me. Let's just sit down together and laugh. We need to get to know each other so much better, and I have the feeling that you may be the one boy who will let me really be myself.

But she caught herself and willed those thoughts away. She forced her way outside, pushing through the bottleneck at the back door. By that time Doug was right behind her. They were near the vine-covered arbor. Page had noticed those boys huddled out in that arbor earlier, laughing and talking. Now the arbor was empty and there was just the sound of the wind.

"Page."

Page kept her back to Doug and stared out

at the acres and acres of grapes. It was dark out there except for the moon and the porch light on Jed's uncle's trailer. She stood stiff as a statue. Doug came up behind her and tried to put his arms around her waist.

She jerked away, as angrily as she'd moved away from Greg.

"What's the matter?" he asked. His voice sounded hurt, confused.

Page grew even angrier. How dare he come after her again and pretend to be pained by her coldness!

"What's going on?"

"Nothing." She forced her voice to sound cool and even. She willed all her feelings back into that icy, hidden place. "Why should anything be going on?"

"Look, Page, I can't talk very long, because Bets — "

"I know about Bets."

"You do? How did you find out?"

"I know more than you think."

"I never said you didn't." He turned away and frowned. "I hope everybody hasn't heard about it."

Page felt as if she were shrinking inside. Doug was practically admitting that his whole relationship with her was a setup.

"Page, I'll be back pretty soon. I have a lot of stuff to tell you."

She was on top of it now. She'd willed her distress into the background. Her brain was coolly figuring how to turn the tables and make Doug look like the fool. "You're coming back?"

"Of course. It's early. Don't you want me to?"

"Not especially."

"What? Come on, Page. Things are definitely weird here." Doug sounded scared. "We can't go back to that again. I thought we figured that out. I can't take it."

"Aw," Page cooed in a baby voice — Whitney's voice. "Why don't you make a big joke out of it, then? You love making jokes. Even if other people don't think you're very funny."

He closed his eyes with great sadness, and for a split second, Page wondered if she wasn't making a terrible mistake.

"Is that what you're trying to say?" he asked shakily. "That this whole thing with you and me is a joke?"

She plastered on her best phony smile. "Haha."

He stood staring at her until Billie Holiday finished her sad verse and the party noise bubbled up again. "Listen, I've gotta take Bets home. Maybe I should call you later."

"Anytime."

Doug hesitated. "What's that supposed to mean?"

Page wasn't sure she knew. The icy part of her was in control, but every time she looked at his face she felt the ice crack. Why did it have to be so confusing and so risky? Was she doing the right thing?

Doug shrugged. "I don't know what the problem is, but maybe we can talk about it later."

"I wouldn't count on it."

"But wait a second. What about. . . ?"

Page made herself do it. She couldn't risk it. She couldn't risk being hurt. "Doug, I've decided everything was a mistake. I don't think we should see each other anymore."

"What?"

Page turned, so she wouldn't have to look. She smelled the grape leaves and felt the breeze, but all her concentration was going into not letting her voice crack. "I just think it's the best thing." She couldn't go any further. She turned and took a step.

"But . . ." Doug sputtered.

He reached out for her hand but Page pushed it away. Then she was running. Running and crying but going as fast as she could. When she finally stopped it was quiet, and Page was alone.

CHAPTER 16

From where Jed sat, in front of the trailer, he could hear the party. The music sounded muffled, but he'd been aware of it all evening. Every once in a while a laugh or a shrill voice punctured the air, forcing him to look across the field at the winery. His uncle's small trailer home wasn't all that far away, but Jed felt like he was living in a hut with a view of the baron's castle.

"So tell me what you think, Jed," Laurel asked. "Please, tell me."

Jed put his strong hands across the hood of his uncle's pickup and boosted himself up. The truck was rusty and faded. When he sat on it some of the old paint invariably ended up on his Levis. But that didn't matter much. For Jed it was a good place to sit and look out over the fields. He'd known that for the last six years, since his mother had left. He was meant to sit out on the hood of an old truck, while the rest of the world went to fancy parties.

"Do what you want to do," Jed finally responded. He pulled a crumpled cigarette pack out of his jacket pocket, even though Laurel hated smoking. He lit up. "Maybe you should go over to Page's party right now," he added, tossing the match in the dirt, "then have all your classmates tell you what you'll need to pack for a summer in Europe."

Laurel looked hurt, but only for a second. She folded her arms. There was a tough look on her face now, and Jed knew it wasn't fake. "They're your classmates, too," she replied. "And I don't even want to go away for the summer." Laurel waved the smoke away, then slapped the truck hood with her palm. The band of Jed's ring rammed into her finger and obviously stung. "Or maybe I do. Maybe part of me does want to go. I don't know. This is like when I was sent back and forth between my dad and my mom. No one lets me decide what I want."

Jed let his hair flop over his eyes. "Don't look at me. I'm not the one who's trying to run your life."

"I'm not so sure about that," Laurel protested. There was anger in her voice tonight that was very different from her usual soft reticence. Jed told himself that it was the sudden news about going away for the summer, and yet he knew this had been building for some time.

"Hey, I'm not the one who tells you what you have to do," he insisted. "It's your dad who's against me. He always has been."

Laurel was leaning against the front of the truck and she bent her head back, as if she wanted to punch the dark sky. "It's both of you!" She sighed and huffed, as if she were trying to say something but it wouldn't quite come out. Finally she blurted out, "Oh, Jed, why did you give me this ring? Does it mean that we're engaged? That now I can't ever go away and leave you? Not even for spring break anymore, let alone all of summer?"

Jed sucked hard on the cigarette. He didn't smoke much anymore and it was making him dizzy. But dizziness was better than thinking about what Laurel had said. The ring. He'd spent all of his savings on it. Every dollar he'd saved. He'd hoped to replace that money with his job on the vineyard. The job he'd screwed up. And the strangest part was that he didn't know what the ring meant, either. He'd just sensed that they had to have some kind of promise. A future together. A future that wouldn't go away, like everything else in his life. If Laurel wore that ring, she would stick with him. No matter what, she wouldn't leave him here, outside and alone.

But he was scared to say that. Instead, he looked at the ground. "I thought you'd like it," he told her.

Laurel faced him, leaned her hands on his knees, and looked up at him. The porch light reflected off her glasses, but he could imagine the intensity of her beautiful green eyes. "I do. I like anything from you. I love you." She paused. "But Jed, you should spend your money on other things." She started to slip the ring off. "Maybe you should take it back."

"Great."

"It's not that I don't like it, it's just too expensive."

"So throw it away."

"Jed!" She pushed the ring securely on her finger and for a moment they listened to the music of the party.

"Please, just keep it," Jed finally whispered. "I'll do something about the money. If it even matters. Everyone else will move on, and I'll be here," he heard himself say. "I'll be moving boxes at this stupid vineyard forever."

Laurel wrapped her arms around his neck, and he pulled her in as hard as he could. He didn't kiss her, because the smell of her hair and the texture of her skin were so overwhelming. It was like making a recording of her to play back when she wasn't with him. Silky, long hair. Hands that pressed hard against the back of his neck. The smell of powder, and art chalk, and thin antique fabric. The deep, full breathing, and the warmth coming from her skin.

They didn't break apart until there was the sound of leaves rustling nearby and the sharp squeal of a cat. Suddenly Big Brother, Jed's uncle's kitten, shot out from under the uneven hedge that bordered the trailer.

"Sorry, cat," they heard a girl say in a sarcastic, empty voice. "I guess it's a night for getting stepped on."

Laurel and Jed sprang further apart — an automatic reflex from the countless times they'd been caught near the creek by the foreman or the hired hands. Jed was embarrassed at his reaction, since he knew that it was just some girl who'd wandered off from the party. And yet there was a quality in the girl's voice that didn't fit with someone out for a carefree stroll.

When he saw who it was he took another step back. It was Page Hain.

"Hello," Page said in a tired, husky voice. She seemed sloppily dressed with her sweatshirt hanging down one shoulder and a twig sticking in her hair. She didn't sound snobby or uptight or any of the things Jed expected. If she'd been stark naked, Jed couldn't have been more aware of how un-Pagelike she seemed. Actually, that's what it was. She seemed naked . . . not in a sexy way, either. Naked as if she'd been stripped of her usual sure exterior. As if she'd come over to see them, knowing that it was a weird thing to do, but just not caring.

They were both startled to see her. There was no point in pretending that this visit was an accident. Page knew the vineyard almost as well as Jed did — and she knew it well enough to have avoided running into him or Laurel for a long time. No, Jed saw something strange in Page's eyes. Maybe it was only that she'd looked at him so directly, or maybe it was the hint that tonight she was an outsider, too. He wasn't sure why or how, but it was clear to him. Rich, beautiful, stuck-up Page Hain was an outsider on her own vineyard at her own party.

"I saw the light on in the trailer," Page whispered to both of them.

Laurel stared, too. Under the flickering porch light Page looked terribly pale. A ghost.

Neither Laurel nor Jed responded. "I was out here and I knew you were here, too," Page said. "I saw you from up there. I always see you. I've wanted to come down and say hello before. But I guess I never did."

"You have?" Laurel said in a very soft voice.

Page shrugged. "I won't bother you." She looked right at Laurel. "I just needed to see somebody that I trusted, somebody that would never use me or set me up." She looked embarrassed at having said so much. "Never mind. I'm being weird. It's a weird night. Maybe I am weird under all my nonweirdness."

"Page, what do you mean?"

She waved her hands, as if her usual way of thinking about things had been tampered with and she was trying to put her thoughts back in order. "I'm going. I have to get back to the party. I just started thinking about when we used to be friends."

Laurel took a step toward her. "I think about it, too. A lot."

For a second Page smiled, and her confused weariness seemed to disappear. She started to walk away.

Laurel called after her. "Page, you don't have to go."

Page turned back. "You don't have to stay out here, either." For a moment the three of them stared at one another. "You could have come up to the party. The whole class was invited."

"That's okay," Jed finally said uneasily. "Parties aren't exactly my style."

Page nodded and looked down into the dark fields. "I understand. Actually, I don't feel like going right back there myself." She started away again, but this time she was headed toward the field rather than back to the house. "I think I need to walk a little. Maybe I'll see you at school. Both of you."

"I'll look for you," Laurel promised.

"Will you?"

Laurel nodded. Page smiled again, then turned and walked off.

The surprise in Jed's stomach didn't leave. "You know what?" he told Laurel.

"What?"

"That's the first time I've seen Page act more like me, than me."

Laurel shook her head. "I know."

Jed sighed.

"Jed," Laurel urged, also gazing down at the rows and rows of grapes. She remembered being a freshman and wandering into that same field. Alone. She stared until Page was no longer visible. So much had changed since then. "We still have each other. We have to remember that. No matter what happens. Even if we can't be together every second. The way we feel about each other won't go away. Don't you think so?"

He put his arms around her and held on as tightly as he could.

It grew very late. Or very early. The sky was becoming a lighter color of gray that made the glow from Bets's flashlight look dimmer. She and Doug were stretched out on her front porch. There was the rustle of the pear tree in the yard and the occasional *mooo* from the cows in the pasture nearby.

"You sure we haven't woken your dad?"

Bets glanced toward her house. The windows were all dark, protected by simple white curtains. "It's okay. If he hasn't come out to yell at us by now, he'll probably sleep until, um, the sun comes up."

"Are you feeling better?"

"I'm starting to. I still feel like such a dope." She'd told Doug all about Kevin and Greg and college and how she just wanted to make some kind of mark for herself. And he'd told her about Page. "What about you?"

"I'm getting there, too." Softly, Doug sang a slow jazz song that began, "Good morning, heartache." Soon he was making up his own lyrics. " 'When you're a junior, don't start hanging around. You have to face things, somehow-ow.' "

They both hummed the tune for a while in very quiet voices. Doug mimed some notes on a pretend saxophone, while Bets leaned back on the stoop and scuffed out a rhythm with her cowboy boot.

"Don't blame Micki," she said when the song was finished.

"How can I? She turned out to be right, didn't she?"

"She's always right."

"Well?"

Bets sat up, hunkering over with her chin propped on her fists. "I wish I was like that. Like you and Micki. Always knowing what to do." She huffed. "And what not to do."

"You think Micki's like that? Or me? Or any of us? You think I'm not a dope, too?"

"Well . . . maybe." Bets smiled. "I just know that this year everybody seems so sure of what they're going to do. Except me."

"Bets, you've always thought that Micki was so far ahead of you. She isn't. She's just different. There are lots of things that you can do that Micki couldn't even touch."

"Sure. Name one."

"Plant a great garden. Build a fence. Ride a horse."

"Big deal."

"Raise lambs."

Bets slapped Doug's shin. She'd won ribbons in 4H when she was younger, but it seemed so dumb now that she didn't want to be reminded of it. "Those things will do me tons of good. I can tell Berkeley about my lambs on my application."

"Bets, everybody's different," Doug sighed, "and you're talking to one of the all-time real weirdos." He sounded sad now. "If you aren't good at the things colleges care about, it's just because you're good at other things instead. You can run, throw, cook — do anything with animals and plants." He picked up a rock and threw it at the pear tree. "And you can't be something that you're not, even if that's what some college wants. And besides, you're pretty good with humans, too."

"How can you say that? After those boys. I've been acting like, you know, such a fool."

"Because you don't play games, or use people. Not that Micki does, either. Not intentionally. But. . . ."

Bets knew he was thinking about Page again. "It's like you said before, um, about Kevin and Greg. If that's the way they treat people, then, well, they're not even worth being upset over. Right?"

"That's another thing you are, Bets. Smart."

Bets laughed.

Doug stretched out, then stood up and began to pace on the edge of the lawn. "You should be doing sports at school, or teaching people to ride, or raising new kinds of sheep."

"First I have to make it past Monday morning. I don't think I can face those guys again."

"Yeah. I know how you feel. I get to see Page in Debate first thing. But who knows, maybe by the time we're seniors she'll be begging me for forgiveness."

"How do we make it until then?"

"Think about other things." Doug leaned back against her. "Lean on our buddies."

"Maybe this whole thing isn't so bad, if it makes me do something about it," Bets reasoned.

"That's another thing about you. You're optimistic."

"Sometimes. You know how hard it is for me

to really talk about stuff, how my thoughts always kind of get mixed up."

"You have a bad enough night, things get very clear." Doug clunked his old Beatle boots together. "Hey, maybe there's a song lyric in that. 'Bad night's over, and the morning looks clear.' " He hummed loudly this time.

"Oh, no."

"What?"

She pointed to her father's window.

"You mean?" He began singing again. " 'Yes, the night's over. I smell the clover. But at least, you are here.' " He held his arms out and started dancing. He pulled Bets up and danced her down the walk toward his car.

"Shhhh!" she giggled.

He spun her. "Do you think my song really did wake up your father?"

"That," she clapped her hand over his mouth and pointed to the sky, "and the fact that the sun's coming up."

The light flicked on in her father's bedroom. Doug kept singing while Bets pushed him into his car. "Shh! Boy am I going to get in trouble."

Plunging in, he accidentally bumped the horn. Sheepishly, he stuck his head out the window and tapped her hand. "That was just to prove that I still can be a clown . . . at very rare moments."

Bets flexed her muscle. "Get out of here before I run you down the road."

Doug started up the engine with a blast. "I'm going. I'm going."

CHAPTER 17

Monday morning. Lockers banging shut. Voices swirling around the halls. Waves, yells, homework being scribbled on the backs of friends. Breakfast on the run. Gym clothes forgotten — some on purpose, some not. Band instruments. New art supplies. Everybody comparing notes on spring break. Some people ecstatic to be back at school. Others moping near their homerooms, complaining that vacation should have lasted a few years longer.

Bets was one of the mopers. It was a rough Monday for her. A paranoid, self-conscious Monday. As she navigated the halls, she was aware of every giggle, every whisper. She slunk. She slipped past the Class of '89 hangouts and took a detour through the freshman lounge. Kids there were young and gangly and unfamiliar. Good. They couldn't know what had happened to her over the break. Trying to keep her courage up, she peered out the windows until she saw the Grizzly mascot painted outside on the gym. She fixed her eye on that determined red bear and kept on going.

"You can do it," she reminded herself. "Um, you can."

She thought back to Micki's pep talk on the phone last night. Who cares about those guys and their stupid macho gossip? Micki had ranted. If they can accuse you of being easy, you can just as well accuse them of the same thing! Last night Bets had understood Micki's logic. Doug had called, too, and between her two friends, Bets decided that she could wrestle this thing. But that was last night. Now it was today, when she had to look people in the face again. When she was going to make her move. Suddenly all of Doug's support and Micki's logic was twisting up in her head like strings of salt-water taffy.

Bets made it out of the freshman lounge and back into the sunny spring air. Clutching her books against her chest, she marched past the Language Labs, the greenhouse, and the Computer Center. Soon she was walking up the gym steps. She almost stopped right there, but turned back telling herself that she'd be late for homeroom. Then she remembered. She'd promised Micki. She'd promised Doug. And even more important, she'd promised herself.

Once inside, she headed straight for the girl's locker room. Usually it was kind of dark and steamy, but after being empty for the last week, it smelled of some kind of cleanser that stung the inside of her nose. The bare concrete clunked under her cowboy boots, and down the corridor she could see the light from Coach Lucht's office. Freshman year she had just been called Mrs. Lucht, but since then Lucht had become a campaigner for girls' team sports, and now she coached girls' basketball, soccer, and softball.

Bets watched the coach behind that funny glass that had wire running through it. She raised her hand to knock, but didn't make contact. Instead, she thought of all the other things that Micki had suggested. Write a book about horses. Collect interviews with local ranchers. Organize a new club. All great Micki ideas that had little appeal for Bets. Meanwhile, Doug came up with wild notions for Bets and the next science fair. Charting the effects of jokes on livestock. The influence of jazz on potted plants. Actually, Doug could probably pull ideas like that off. But Bets had to start with something that was really right for her.

Bets was about to really pound the door this time, when she saw that Lucht was smiling at her and motioning her in.

"Oh. Um. Okay."

Bets opened the door and walked in the stuffy little office. She'd stood at the door to this office plenty of times, waiting for the equipment room key or Band-aids or iodine, but she'd never been inside before. The walls were covered with game schedules, photos of some of the athletes who'd competed at the Winter Olympics that year in Calgary, a few ribbons, and snapshots of Coach Lucht's family.

"Hi, Betsy. What are you doing here so early?"

"Um, hi. Are you busy or anything?"

The coach put her pencil down, swung around in her chair, and folded her arms. "Not too busy."

"Oh. Do you think I could maybe, well, talk to you?"

"What's on your mind?"

"Okay." Bets tried to put her thoughts in order. She stared at the floor. "Um, I was, uh, just thinking about, you know, myself and wanting to do something more at school. See, well, I've been thinking about how I'm almost a senior, and I guess I feel like I haven't done anything too important here, so when I think about college, or whatever I'm going to do after high school, it makes me feel pretty unprepared and scared and stuff."

"Yes?" Lucht looked baffled.

Bets, who usually had to fight to connect her brain to her mouth, suddenly couldn't stop talking. "So I thought I'd start by doing something in sports. I'm good at sports, um, at least I think I am — "

"You are," the coach interrupted.

"Oh. Right. Thanks. So, I know that, like, the softball tryouts already happened and everything, but I wanted to see if maybe I could be with the team anyway. Learn about coaching maybe, or just help out. Anything."

"That's all you want, Betsy?"

"Yeah. I guess. Is that okay?"

"Just to help the team? To do anything?"

Bets bit her lip. Now that she was here, was she going to offer to be the water carrier? That was the kind of thing she used to do and that was fine for an underclassman. But that was probably why she'd gotten into this predicament in the first place. Now that she was a junior she had to do more, more than back up Micki or make spaghetti for her friends. She had to show those boys she commanded more respect than a one-night stand. She had to show herself that she was a person who should be respected. "Well, do you think I could try out late for the varsity team?"

There, she had said it. Bets felt like a wild animal had just escaped from her mouth. There was no reining it in now. She nervously looked around the room again, wishing it weren't quite so small, and there weren't so many windows. That way no one could see her face when the coach said no.

Coach Lucht tipped back in her chair and shook her head. "Betsy Frank. You nut. Why have you waited so long? You should have been competing since you were a freshman."

"I should?"

"I mentioned the soccer team to you freshman year and you acted like I wanted to ship you off to Siberia. I'm not allowed to push athletes into trying out for teams if they don't want to."

Bets thought back to freshman soccer. All

195

she'd been thinking about that semester was Micki's feud with Page. "I guess I've changed since then."

"I guess you have."

"So, um, what do you think?"

Coach Lucht pondered for a moment. At last she stuck out her hand to shake. "Betsy, I've seen you in class for three years," she said, "and I know we could use you on the team. I think it would be a good idea for you to learn about coaching, too. Our next practice is tomorrow after school."

"You mean I can try out?"

"I mean, you're on the team. Be there."

Bets wanted to cry again, to babble incoherently, to hug Coach Lucht, and throw her books in the air. Instead, she returned the teacher's firm grip and said in a sure, clear voice, "Thank you. I'll be there. Suited up and ready, tomorrow."

Bets left the gym like a dignified upperclass person. She managed to wait until she was halfway to her homeroom before she started singing and leaping and giggling to herself.

On the other side of campus, in Steinberg's beginning debate class, Micki was feeling some Monday morning icks of her own. She'd expended so much energy over the weekend — instilling confidence in Bets . . . cheering up Doug — she hadn't really prepared herself to see Page again.

But as soon as she walked into debate, the first person she laid eyes on was Page. The classroom was buzzing with excess vacation energy, and Page was the only one sitting at her desk, her perfect face buried in her notebook. Micki avoided the noisy reunions and stared at Page. Not that it was unusual for Page to be in class early, studying or going over a debate strategy. But today, something about Page was very different.

Micki had expected Page to return to school in triumph, like some comic-book villainess. But if anything, Page seemed more fragile than before. Her stiff authority had turned vague. Two brambles clung to the hem of her jumper, and her dark braid looked slept on. In fact, for the first time that Micki could remember, Page looked like a spacy, slightly sad, but normal junior.

When Doug and Thompson rushed in right before the bell, Micki made even stranger observations — ones that made her feel as if a spring was uncoiling inside her. First it was Thompson, looking at her with his ultraintelligent eyes, and giving her an understanding smile. Then it was Doug, trying so hard to avoid looking at Page that he almost fell over a row of desks. And Page seemed equally pained at being in the same room with Doug. She did other things that Micki didn't associate with Page Hain. She accidentally knocked over her books. She bit her fingernails.

"Okay, everybody. Settle down. Vacation is over and reality has returned," Mr. Steinberg announced after the bell. He looked rested and ready to go, even though the class was still groaning and talking. After taking roll, he put on his let's-get-serious face and pointed to the debate instructions that covered the blackboard.

Mr. Steinberg explained how each side would present a simple argument, with one rebuttal following. Another student would judge the outcome and give reasons for their decision. This was somewhat simpler than real competitive debating, he told them, but it was a start.

The topic selected: Should One *Always* Tell the Truth, and Nothing But the Truth? Mr. Steinberg grinned when he told them. "It seems to me a very relevant topic, not only for people your age, but for people in politics. Remember we have a Presidential election coming up next fall. Those of you interested in school politics should be most interested in this debate." He looked at Micki and Page, and then at Thompson. Thompson was the only one to return the teacher's smile.

"Now for the first team." Mr. Steinberg looked down at the attendance sheet and then out at the rows of chairs. "Ms. Hain, you will argue the affirmative."

Page looked up from her desk. She seemed to have not quite comprehended what it was Mr. Steinberg was saying. The fuzzy expression that she had worn from the beginning of class was still there.

Fuzzy or not, Micki was afraid of her. Something told her that she would be selected as Page's opponent. She was usually picked first — she was one of Mr. Steinberg's favorites because she was always willing to give him an argument.

But if there was one person Micki *didn't* want to argue with today, it was Page.

"And, let's see. Who else? Ms. Greene, I think I will ask for your participation." Micki gave Thompson a save-me look. Steinberg caught it. "What? I thought you'd be raring to go. Too much spring vacation?"

Micki couldn't answer, but she wanted to say, Yes, that's it exactly. Too much spring vacation, and I'm not in the mood to face off with Page Hain. Instead, she slowly got up from her desk and came toward the front of the class where the two podiums stood.

"Finally," Mr. Steinberg went on, "one more participant. Let's see. Someone different. Someone with a different point of view. Ah, yes. Mr. Markannan, you seem perfect. You always have a different way of seeing the world."

"No, thanks," Doug blurted out, trying to sound more casual than Micki knew he was feeling. "I'll get slaughtered." He pointed at Micki and Page. "Those two up there are the all-time great arguers." He pretended to crawl under his desk, and everyone laughed. Micki wondered if she was the only one who knew how serious he was. Besides her, only Thompson seemed concerned.

"Well, you must hone your skills," Steinberg said in a corny voice. "Hone your skills. That way you'll be able to defend yourself, Mr. Markannan."

Doug slowly got up from his desk. This was a very different Doug from the one who usually couldn't wait to get up and show off. The three of them took their places at the head of the class. Page and Doug stood far away from one another, as if they wished they could be in separate rooms.

"Now," Mr. Steinberg said. "Page has the affirmative, so Doug, you take the negative."

Micki was startled into looking up. Doug was going to debate Page! She saw the flash of surprise and distress that passed back and forth from Doug to Page, and then back to her.

"Michelle, I want you to be the judge. You enforce the rules and keep track of the time."

"Me?"

"Page, you'll begin."

"Okay," Micki said as soon as Page was at the podium. She held up her watch. "Start."

Page fixed her eyes on the posters covering the back wall, took a deep breath, and began in a shaky voice. "Truth. There is no such thing as a half-truth, or part of the truth. There is only one truth. One way of seeing things. Either something is true, and can be proven so, or it is a lie." The corners of her mouth were trembling slightly, but she pushed through her opening statement. "Truth is one of the standards we use to judge things by. In a courtroom we are asked to tell the truth and nothing but the truth. Our concept of truth is secure and unshakable. Truth is a value we uphold. Therefore, we must keep that value as something pure and constant. Always."

"Time," Micki managed, letting Page know her opening statement was up. Page flashed her steely eyes ever so briefly at Doug, then backed up against the blackboard. "Opening statement from the negative, please," Micki announced.

Doug took a step forward. Usually he started his arguments with a big gesture or a joke, but this morning he merely cleared his throat and stared down at his Beatle boots. "Okay. What is the truth? Anyone who argues that the truth is a definite thing, that there is only one truth, is simply wrong. Truth is relative to everything else around it. It changes all the time. If I played my saxophone full blast in this room right now, people would say that it was loud. And that would be true. But if a lot of people were talking, or if a jack hammer was going outside, you might ask me to play louder because it would be true that my saxophone would sound too quiet. And that would also be true."

"Time."

Doug seemed relieved to be off the spot, but Page didn't wait for Micki to reintroduce her. She pushed her shoulders back, unaware of the smudges of chalk dust on her jumper. The look on her face grew even more stubborn.

"What my opponent is referring to," Page pressed, "has nothing to do with real truth. If we were to measure the loudness or softness of his saxophone with a noise meter, it would give us a 'true' answer, and it wouldn't change, no matter what else was going on in the room. Mr. Markannan has proved my point, not his. When we discuss whether or not one should always tell the truth, we must realize that there is only one truth to tell. Truth that can be measured, photographed, proved. And it doesn't change, no matter what else is going on around it."

"I disagree," Doug blurted.

Micki made a move to stop him. She was supposed to announce each section, and make sure that things continued in an orderly fashion. "Doug, you may offer a rebuttal." Mr. Steinberg was watching carefully from the back of the room. He was clearly as interested in this debate as the rest of the class was.

Doug began again. "Ms. Hain has proved my point, not hers. For example, you could take a picture of someone stealing a car stereo, you could even see that person with your own eyes break into a car, take tools out of their coat pocket, and go to work. But how would you really know they were stealing? How would you know that it wasn't their own car?"

"But at a certain point you put things together!" Page interrupted. Her perfect face was starting to look reddish and bunched up. She caught herself breaking the rules and looked back at Micki.

"Affirmative may give rebuttal," Micki said.

Page jumped back in. "If everyone tells you that a certain person is a thief, and then you see that person break into a car and start pulling out the car stereo, then he's probably stealing. You rely on your experience, your common sense — "

Doug was starting to look as frazzled as Page. "Neither of which have anything to do with truth!"

Mr. Steinberg began pacing across the back of the room. "Keep your heads on," he coached. "You both have good arguments. Don't let your emotions get in the way. Micki, give them each another round."

Doug didn't wait for Micki to give him the go-ahead. "Let me go back to Ms. Hain's point about finding the truth from what other people say. If that's how you judge the truth, by gossip and hearsay, then there's no such thing as truth. Of course, from what I know of Ms. Hain, the real truth has never been very important. She just admitted that she lets other people tell her what the truth is."

"That isn't what I meant! We all have to have some kind of standard," Page pleaded. "Mr. Markannan seems to think that everyone can do whatever they want, and then decide for themselves what is real and true."

Micki knew that logic was disappearing, and that this could turn into a personal free-for-all, which was against every debate precept. But there was this awful, frightened feeling deep in her stomach that left her unable to step in.

"And why shouldn't I decide for myself?" Doug provoked. "At least I'm not so uptight that I freak out if everything isn't exactly the way I think it should be."

"Oh, I suppose everything is my fault." Page's face was so flushed that she looked as if she were on fire. "After the way you lied to me — "

"You were the one who led me on!"

"I never lied to you!" Page started laughing. An out-of-control, furious laugh. "It's funny, you know that?"

Micki stared at Page. Everyone was staring. As class president, Page had given dozens of speeches and presentations. And she'd always been the model of decorum and control. Why, all of a sudden, was she acting like someone from the drama department? But before Micki could interfere, Mr. Steinberg stepped in.

"That's enough!" he said sharply, raising both hands. "I let you go on because I thought you were both onto good strategies. But you're not sticking to your points. You're all over the place. Keep your personal feelings out of this class. Debate is a controlled argument. Not chaos. Take your seats."

Slowly, the three of them returned to their chairs. Micki's heart was pounding. She stared down at her notebook, too embarrassed to look Mr. Steinberg, or anyone else in the face. She knew exactly why Doug and Page had gotten out of control, and why she had been unable to interrupt them. It was simple. Too simple. They had both been straight and honest with one another. She was the one who had lied.

Thompson and two other juniors got up to show the class the correct way of arguing your points, but Micki barely heard them. Too much else was swirling around her head. How had she known that Page was using Doug? What proof did she really have, other than some old lying reflex of hers that distrusted Page and that said that Doug was a clown? But Doug wasn't really a clown anymore. He was handsome, talented, bright, and sure he was goofy and offbeat, but people found that part of him most charming of all. She'd done it. She ruined things for Doug. She'd wounded Page almost as viciously as she had two years ago, when she'd graffitied Page's locker. Just as deviously as Page had worked last year to ruin Micki's reputation with her class.

Micki was still filled with her realization when the class ended. As soon as the bell rang, the early morning hubbub bubbled up again. For most of them, it was almost as if the class hadn't happened, and they went right back to the how-I-spent-my-spring-vacation stories. All of them were talking about the reunions and having contests to see who had the deepest tan.

Quickly, avoiding Doug and Page, Micki scurried out to the hall. She would have been home-free, except that Thompson caught her. He was right behind her, as if he'd read her mind and was waiting to confront her.

Micki looked at him and thought, Oh, no, I can't face Thompson, too. I can't have him hate me, too, and know that I've done an impulsive and dishonest thing.

"Don't bug me, Thompson," she mumbled. "I'm not having a good day."

Thompson stood close, looking at her intently. "Maybe I can help out a little."

"I doubt it." Micki pounded the wall behind her. "I'm the know-it-all, aren't I. Or the don't-know-anything-at-all."

Thompson nudged her. "As much as I enjoy hearing it, don't be too hard on yourself." He stuck his hands in his pockets and stared down at his deck shoes. "I assume you are referring to that rather unusual debate between Page and our man Doug."

"You assume I'm referring to them. . . . Please, Thompson, just come to the point. I'm a jerk and I hurt one of my best friends. I helped all those lies between them. I know, you told me so."

"I did, didn't I."

"Oh, Thompson, please. Don't. I feel so awful."

He reached up and gently swept her wispy hair away from her face. "I know you do. That's one of things I really like about you. You care."

"About me? You don't think I'm horrible?"

"If I thought you were horrible, would I spend this much energy driving you crazy?"

Micki suddenly felt as if her feet were slipping out from under her. "I don't know." She had that frothy feeling again, and tried to cover it. "So should I do something to get them back together?"

"I think they have to figure it out on their own."

"Will they?"

"Maybe. Who knows?"

"I just wish I'd kept my big mouth shut."

"I like your big mouth." He grinned. "Everybody makes mistakes. Even me."

"Nooo."

"Well, rarely."

Micki spun around, catching him in the stomach with her arm. He twisted her into an armlock, and whispered in her ear, "Admit it. You like me. You have for a long time. My many good qualities have finally gotten to you."

Micki started laughing and trying to twist away. "Forget it," she giggled. "No way."

Thompson had her all the way around the waist now. "Admit it." He hugged her harder. "You're crazy about me."

Micki threw back her head until she felt his cheek close against hers. "All right! I admit it. I like you! I like you a lot."

He let her go and started back down the hall. "I know." He jumped over a bench, blew her a kiss, and jogged onto the lawn.

Micki watched him go and stuck her hands on her hips. "Ooh," she gloated to herself, "you are so predictable."

CHAPTER 18

Laurel rushed out of her art class. Late. Seventh period had ended twenty minutes ago. But her whole funky Monday had been off-schedule . . . bumpy . . . full of surprises that kept throwing her off the mark.

First, her dad had insisted on driving her to school. In the middle of a left turn, he suddenly stared at her hand and almost drove the car onto the center divider. Then, of course, he had pulled over to ask when Laurel had started wearing that ring, and where it had come from. By the time the discussion was over, Laurel was reeling and late to homeroom.

After that came Page. She was waiting at Laurel's locker at midmorning break. Laurel wasn't aware that Page even knew where her locker was this year, but there Page was saying she wanted to say hello, to chat about the weird way she'd acted in debate. How she felt like she *should* care that she'd been so weird, but she didn't. By the time that strange conversation was over, Laurel was even more off balance. She was also tardy to English.

Now it was after school and Laurel was trying to get an idea for a new cartoon . . . while at the same time worrying about Jed. Laurel usually stayed after for a few minutes, finishing things up in Mrs. Foley's art room. And usually Jed met her there. But today he didn't come. Today, when she wanted to make sure that things were really okay between them . . . when she wanted to tell him about her father . . . and she wanted to tell him about Page, Jed had disappeared.

Finally, she closed her sketch pad and headed into the hall. The sun was still eye-squinting bright and there was a damp warmth that reminded her of summer. Right away she saw Micki, Thompson, Doug, and Bets hanging out on the lawn.

"LAUREL!" they all seemed to shout at the same time.

Laurel met them on the lawn and helped Micki up. "Have any of you seen Jed?"

Four pairs of eyes checked with one another, then four heads shook and said no.

"Where are you all going?"

"There's this big volleyball game planned over at the courts," Doug told her. "It kind of got organized at lunch. The weather's so good. It's the official it's-not-really-back-to-school contest. Those who believe against those who don't."

"I'm not going, though," Bets insisted.

When Laurel had seen Bets at lunch, Bets had been flying with excitement about making the softball team. Now she plopped down on the grass, as if she were starting a sit-down strike.

"If I can go face everyone," Doug lectured Bets, "you can do it, too."

"Those guys will be there, I just know it." Bets buried her face in her hands.

Doug swooped down behind her and scooped her up. "Everyone knows I got the royal dumpola at that party. And I'm probably going to get an F in debate from Mr. Steinberg, and I managed not to talk to Page once after that." Doug grinned. "I'm still alive."

"Yeah, but you're insane."

"True. Let's go."

Micki and Doug finally got Bets up and, following Thompson, they headed toward the playing fields. Laurel went, too. The playing courts bordered the parking area for mopeds and motorcycles, so she could at least check for Jed's motorbike.

They walked around the outside of the gym, past where the baseball team was practicing and some girls were lifting weights in the sun. Laurel could see the gang of upperclassmen collecting around the volleyball courts, but she hung back and let the foursome go on without her. She stopped. She'd spotted Jed, coasting on his bike, swinging one leg off as he pulled it into the parking rack. Laurel clutched her sketch pad to her chest and ran to meet him.

"Where were you?" she asked. "I waited in Mrs. Foley's room."

"I had to go downtown." Jed wiped sweat from his upper lip with the back of his hand. Laurel watched his woven bracelet slip up and down his tanned arm.

"When?"

He turned away to lock up his bike. "I cut last period."

Laurel didn't say anything. She knew that Jed would always have his own way of doing things, just like she did.

"I went to see this friend of my uncle's." Jed turned to look at her. "The one who used to own the warehouse where I used to work on my sculptures."

"Why?"

He stared down at her hand, saw that the ring was still there, and smiled. "About a summer job. He runs a gas station now. The Mobil station on East Main."

"What did he say?"

"He thinks he can use me." He kicked the bike tire. "It's just a crummy, greasy job. But at least it's not on the vineyard."

Laurel dropped her sketch pad and books on the asphalt and threw herself against him. "It's not a crummy job. It's great."

He hugged her with desperate hardness, then peeled her arms away from his neck. He took hold of her hand and fingered the ring.

"I won't take it off," she promised him.

"Good."

"My dad finally saw it."

"What did he say?"

"That I'm going away for the summer. Definitely. I don't have a choice."

"I figured that."

They leaned against each other, gazing at the crowd that had collected around the volleyball net. Kids were practicing slamming the ball over the net, while someone turned on a radio and a senior boy showed off by walking on his hands. A few girls were making a volleyball passing machine, the sort of stunt they hadn't pulled since they were silly freshmen.

"Our class," Jed said, shaking his head. "Did you see Page today?"

"Yes." Laurel searched the volleyball crowd for Page, but didn't see her. She had the feeling that Jed was looking for Page, too.

"It'll be okay," Jed said finally. "Summer. Pumping gas. I'm not the only person who feels like an outsider in this town, you know."

Laurel thought of telling him she knew that very well. After all, in some ways she was outside things, too. And yet, she knew somehow that he wasn't talking about her.

"I just thought about that a lot. Sometimes I feel like I'm the only person who has a hard time, I guess. But I'm not." He got a philosophical look. "Everybody has to deal with their own stuff."

"Yes."

They entwined arms — woven bracelets, denim jackets, both matched up. They stood there together and watched the game.

* * *

"Just look them right in the eyes," Micki was advising Bets.

Thompson had been picked captain of the I-believe-it's-back-to-school team. He was about to pick his team, and he paced up and down the court, examining the potential players as if he were a drill sergeant.

"Oh, Micki," Bets gasped, grabbing Micki's arm and trying to hide behind her.

Micki saw them, too — Kevin and Greg in the midst of a circle of guys, slapping each others' backs and making jokes. Greg was the captain of the nonbeliever team.

"I don't want to be here," Bets swore. "I don't want to see those guys ever again."

"Hurry up and pick teams," yelled Sam Pond. He was seconded by the Dubrosky twins and Paul O'Conner.

Thompson grinned and looked around, deciding who to pick for his first player. Pointing like the needle on a dial, he finally stopped right at Bets. "Betsy Frank, I want you for my team."

Right away the dirty laughter started, and Bets took a step back.

Micki wanted to slug Greg and Kevin. Bets looked like she wished she could die on the spot. Actually Micki was partly furious at Thompson for picking Bets first and putting her in the spotlight. In fact, part of her wanted to march over and drag Thompson off the court. But there was another part of her that was starting to trust him. She had the odd feeling that he was up to something, that he had their best interests at heart.

"Go on," Micki urged Bets. "It'll be okay."

Thompson threw the ball to Bets and pointed her to the number-one serving position. It was Greg's turn to pick, but he was too busy making cracks with the guys.

Thompson interrupted. "What are you talking about, Greg?" he prodded. More macho laughs and elbow jabs. "Share it with all of us if it's so funny."

The guys exploded with laughter. Finally Sam Pond blurted, "We just think you might have a secret reason for your number-one draft pick."

Thompson's intelligent eyes shone with quiet anger. "Do you? You think I should have picked one of you athletic geniuses?"

They busted up again. "We think you may be thinking a little too much about what you want to do after the game." More gruff ha-has and whispers.

Micki was about to drag Bets off the court, when Thompson suddenly made a beeline in her direction.

"Are you questioning my wisdom for picking a girl first for my team?" he said, in a very know-it-all Thompson way.

The guys laughed even louder.

Thompson told the whole crowd, "If I wanted to do that, I wouldn't have asked her to be the first person to serve. I'd just do this." He suddenly pulled Micki out onto the court, and leaned her over, as if they were in the middle of an exotic tango. And then, with everyone looking on in total shock, he kissed her.

For a second, Micki was so stunned that she went limp as a piece of overdone asparagus. But then she felt a surge of such joy and energy that she wanted to stay there, kissing Thompson in the middle of a volleyball court forever. She wrapped her arms around Thompson's neck, leaned him over in the other direction, and kissed him back.

There were catcalls and whistles and applause. Greg and Kevin seemed a little confused. Their thunder had been taken away, their macho bragging had been upstaged by Thompson and Micki, and no one cared anymore that they were laughing or spreading gossip. Suddenly all the attention had been diverted from Bets to Thompson and Micki.

"Well, Thompson," she said, when they finally separated. She was barely able to breathe. "I guess I can't call you predictable anymore." She bowed to everyone, and then staggered off the court.

The picking of the teams went pretty fast after that. And so did the play. By the end of the first game, Bets had spiked, served, and volleyed brilliantly. She led her team to a quick win. Kevin and Greg were left sprawling on the asphalt, trying to return her points.

"Hey, Betsy," Doug called out, "I think I know another thing you're good at."

"Me, too," Bets answered, and then she grinned at Doug. "And I bet you there's a lot more."

The ball went up and floated over the net.

By five the game was over. Team practices had broken up. The sun was fading, the janitors were swabbing the hall floors, and Doug was still replaying Bets's triumph in his head. Every time Kevin or Greg had tried anything on the court, Bets had been right there, slamming the volleyball down their macho throats and scoring one for Thompson's team. By the end, Greg and Kevin had practically limped off the court.

"Good for you, Bets," Doug sighed to himself. He was glad that his friends were feeling more settled. Bets. Micki and Thompson. Even Laurel and Jed, watching from the sidelines. They all seemed more at peace. He was the only one still in the twilight zone.

He was crossing the main lawn, dodging the sprinklers, on the way to his locker. He tried to make himself think about European history, or his upcoming project for Thorson's computer class. But his thoughts went even further into the ozone. Because just as he turned the corner and walked past the door of Mrs. Freeman's creative writing room, he found himself looking right at Page.

She was coming from the direction of the library, a tall stack of books under her arm. She looked more put together than she had that morning in debate class, and yet something about the way she moved was still a little vague and un-Page-like. He considered avoiding her. He hadn't spoken to her since Steinberg's class. But as strongly as he ordered his legs to march in the other direction, he found himself cutting across the walkway until he was right in Page's path.

For a moment he thought she would pretend

not to see him and keep walking. But she stopped and stood very still, hugging her books with her head down.

"Yo," he said, not quite looking at her. Then there was a long silence, during which not a single coherent thought came into his head. It was as if he were temporarily possessed, as if someone were sending odd, conflicting messages into his brain, messages that he couldn't understand.

"What are you doing here so late?" Page finally asked.

"Huh? Oh. Volleyball. This dumb volleyball game. Actually, it wasn't dumb at all, for some people." He felt more tongue-tied than Bets. "What about you?"

She shifted and took a quick, shallow breath. "I stayed after to apologize to Mr. Steinberg. For . . . this morning. Then I did some research on a new debate strategy."

"Oh, a new strategy. Better get one right away. You wouldn't want people to talk." He put on a phony announcer's voice. *"Page Hain lost her strategy this morning. She's turned into a lose-your-strategy kind of girl."* He didn't want to make fun of her, especially since he could see her stiffen in response. But he didn't know what else to say. He sighed, "I guess you could use a new one. Me, too."

"I guess so."

They stood there for another agonizing moment. Finally Page turned on her heel and began to leave.

"Page, wait!" Doug blurted. He hadn't been

able to put this whole thing together. There was a part of him that sensed that what had happened between them had been real and true and terrific, and that the rest had just been a misunderstanding. But he wasn't sure how to clarify things, to go back to the beginning, to reverse the hurt that had happened.

Page had turned back and there was a flash of hope in her eyes. "Yes?"

He stared.

"Yes?"

"What?"

"You wanted to tell me something?" she prompted.

Everything, Doug thought to himself. I want to tell you everything. But for once, not a sound came out of his mouth.

Page waited until a pair of noisy seniors burst down the hall. Then she put her together, presidential face back on and stood very straight. "I'll see you in class, then."

"See you in class," Doug echoed.

She waited one last stretched-out moment, then turned and slowly walked away.

Doug stood, paralyzed, watching her. Her stride was purposeful now. Controlled and quick. Doug wondered if two such different people were ever meant to be together. He wondered if he and Page should ever have been together in the first place. And he couldn't help wondering if they might never be together again.

CLASS of 89

SENIOR

A hush came over the crowd, reminding Doug of the time he'd seen *The Ten Commandments* on TV. But this hush wasn't awe-inspired. Doug could tell that most seniors were totally intimidated at Page's idea of having their prom at a private country club—which wouldn't let nine-tenths of their parents through their imposing brass doors.

"Does anyone want more information about the club?" Page asked. Her voice sounded a little embarrassed, as if she knew as well as Doug how out of place a lot of her classmates would feel at a place like that.

Paul O'Conner piped up from the back, "I just know they fine you if you try to cut across the golf course."

Page looked unsure. "It's just an idea. I thought we should at least vote on it. Does anyone want to say anything?"

Caroline lectured, "Page and I have already discussed this privately. But I just want to say to the rest of you that we can either have a prom to remember — we can either be winners and go out in style — or we might as well forget the whole thing."

The class had become even quieter, and Doug had the feeling that Caroline was bullying them. The weird part was that Caroline's family wasn't rich. The rumor was that her parents would sacrifice anything so that their brilliant daughter could get ahead.

Page was looking more and more unsure. "We'd better take a vote."

Doug nudged Micki. "I can't stand this."

"I know. I know." Micki was with him all the way. "It's pathetic. The whole end of our senior year is going to be like this."

Doug leaned toward Micki and joked, "Well, if it were up to me, we'd have the prom at the Rat Club."

Micki stared at him. "Where?"

"It's a joke."

"No, what did you say?"

"The Rat Club. I was kidding, Mick."

"Wait." Micki's eyes were suddenly as bright as the hot pink sweatshirt she wore over her yellow print jumper. "Doug!"

"What?"

"That's brilliant."

Doug frowned. He wanted a prom that rocked, but the Rat Club? The Rat Club wasn't a suggestion, it was an out-and-out challenge.